Universal Power of Alphabetical Series

Universal Power of Alphabetical Series

A self-guide workbook to innovate your ordinary self into X—ordinary self

Kanika Sinha

Library of Congress Control Number:		2018914328
ISBN:	Hardcover	978-1-9845-7044-4
	Softcover	978-1-9845-7043-7
	eBook	978-1-9845-7042-0

Print information available on the last page.

Rev. date: 03/30/2019

To order additional copies of this book, contact:
Xlibris
1-888-795-4274
www.Xlibris.com
Orders@Xlibris.com
787976

CONTENTS

DEDICATION

TO THE "DREAMER in you" who can be a child, teenager, youngster and an adult too as "Age Doesn't Matter" and who dreams to innovate the better or best version then yesterday to experience the next level of growth and success so as to change or improve the taste, quality and dimensions of their current life and to inspire people at large irrespective of any age and stage of life believing that –

DREAMS neither has any standard size nor shape because dreams are dreams and also doesn't have any expiration date so, we should keep trying until we start living all our dreams in REALITY because,

Dreams are not the one which you saw in sleep,
Dreams are the one which don't let you sleep,
So, dare to dream and have courage to make them true,
As, the secret to happiness is freedom but
secret to freedom is courage!

And, also to my family and those inspirational personalities whose powerful words boosted my optimistic spirit and empowered me to share my life story and learning experiences with the dreamers in the outside world too especially, with those parents who wants to guide their children from much early or middle school age to help them experience the real taste of meaningful life as early as possible and can help them to start living their dreams into reality as early as they can to utilize their precious time in much optimum ways.

ACKNOWLEDGMENT

I would like to express my deepest gratitude to all my wonderful Family, Friends, Instagram and Facebook followers who expressed their love and support throughout my journey of exploration while finding my deepest passion and highest purpose of life and I really hope that my true passion and highest purpose of life should help you too to find your true passion and highest purpose of life to live a meaningful life ahead to live your life with the fullest enthusiasm always, always, and always.

INTRODUCTION

A S A DREAMER, an Explorer, Learner, an Adventurer, an Artist, Motivational Writer, an Educator and your Life Coach, I aim at helping those friends who are looking to improve the quality and taste of their life then yesterday believing –

> *"There is no perfect time to realize your true potentials to convert any of your dreams into reality but sooner the better is always a good decision to get started with the right doings" (Kanika Sinha)*

Also, please remember that, there would never be the perfect moment other than the one you are living right now because, the moment you are living right now is the only right moment that you have in your hand to do things that you want or wanted to do to live your life with fullest enthusiasm always.

Just do what you love, to make every moment as the perfect moment forever.

Live in the moment and when you are living in the moment simply, live in the moment and do not dwell in the past, do not dream of the future, just concentrate the mind on the present moment to make the next moment right.

And, the moment you realize your true potentials that moment of realization will become perfect time for you as each individual is unique and has a different way of living the life.But to be able to achieve what you truly deserve, you should have some life success mantra that will help you to achieve the dream life you want to design and live all your way.

Do you have any Life Success Mantra, to keep yourself motivated or driven in life all the time when you are trying to achieve something new in your life or travel to a place you have never been before?

If Yes, it's awesome but if No, just don't worry as you can have deep faith in my success mantra as it really does wonders to help you shape your "SELF" and "LIFE" in better ways believing –

"Better the Self, Better the Life" (Kanika Sinha)

So, my Life Mantra says -

You will be victorious in anything or everything
if you love doing it just keep the PASSION alive
(Kanika Sinha)

And, if you too believe so, let me ask you some quick questions -

Are you a Dreamer because every great dream begins with a dreamer?

Are you an Explorer?

Are you an Immortal Learner?

Are you an Adventurer?

Are you a Passionate Soul who is wanting to experience the next level of growth and success in something you either like or love doing?

Are you wanting to do something for the universe as well apart from doing everything for your family and friends as your social responsibility?

If the answer is yes, to all the above questions than, how would you like to contribute is the question that came to my mind when I wanted to do something for my family, friends and the universe at large and to answer that I asked lot many questions to myself because I was not able to decide what could be the best life path for myself to live a meaningful life ahead to make use of my creative energies in best possible creative ways thinking -

Whatever I choose to do, should create some kind of optimistic energies in some form to be used by someone else in the universe to work like helping hand during their darkest or hardest time of life.

So, here are all those questions that I asked to myself before deciding best life path for myself -

Are you dreaming to become a Choreographer because you see a Dancer in you?

Are you dreaming to become a Singer because you see a Singer in you?

Are you dreaming to become a Musician because you see a Musician in you?

Are you dreaming to become a Sketcher because you see a Sketcher in you?

Are you dreaming to become a Painter because you see a Painter in you?

Are you dreaming to become an Author because you see a Writer in you?

Are you dreaming to become a Speaker because you see a Speaker in you?

Are you dreaming to become an Actor because you see a Model in you?

Are you dreaming to become a Photographer because you see a Photographer in you?

Are you dreaming to become an Educator because you see a compassionate teacher in you?

Are you dreaming to become a World Class Chef because you love cooking for your loved ones on everyday basis as Home Chef?

Are you dreaming to become Home Décor and Interior Artists because you love decorating your own house? or

Are you dreaming to become something else because the list look endless?

Well, if the answer is yes, to all the above questions, you can do or achieve anything you want, is something what I told to myself provided, I should try making use of some special ingredients to cook the delicious dream life recipe with patience and perseverance just the way we cook delicious authentic food for our loved ones patiently on everyday basis without any excuse despite of the efforts this activity demands to keep ourself mentally and physically healthy above all other challenges of life.

But, before converting any of your dream recipe into reality and before changing the taste of your life, what critically important is, to know, understand and shape our *Self* deeply or to have self – awareness and, to do that we should explore, enlighten, educate and empower ourself so much that we should be able to guide other people honestly to help them live their life peacefully as a way of living spiritual purpose of life.

Since, I wanted to explore my deepest self by pursuing all of my interest areas so that I can convert some of my passionate hobbies into some kind of profitable profession hence, knowing and understanding my deepest self became critically important for me so, I decided to spend quality time on myself patiently on everyday basis without any excuse to keep myself happy and content to avoid feelings of regret at any later stage of my life.

And, as a result of investing time, energy, money and hope, I gained some wisdom to develop a simple language to be understood by all in an easygoing way to form deepest connection on compassionate ground wherever we all are in this world.

So, Do you LOVE cooking as an ART being a big-time foodie? or

LIKE cooking as the necessity of life because we are bound to cook for xyz reasons on everyday basis?

Either way we are deeply involved in cooking as an unavoidable activity of daily life to keep ourself healthy.

Either way we are continuously feeding our mind, heart and soul with essential nutrients or ingredients or optimistic energies on everyday basis to keep ourselves healthy and wealthy all our life.

But, have you ever thought about the wisdom this activity can teach us in the most unique way which, when is applied in any sphere of our life, our life can become more meaningful, beautiful and powerful then yesterday because the amount of PATIENCE and HARDWORK this one activity demands above all other daily challenges of life to feed our loved ones, no other household activity does. Right?

Yes, I too agree with it, this one activity can give us that kind of universal wisdom or powers to break our mental limits which no other household activity can do.

Would you like to know about that wisdom?

Let's take a look.

Everything that is cooked inside your kitchen is the gift that you receive from Mother Nature or Universe on daily basis in the most authentic or organic way so that you can feed your soul with versatile natural flavors in your daily life before creating something special for your loved ones.

But, when we try to do something special, some special ingredients also goes into that authentic recipe in the form of special spices or herbs bringing extra delicious flavors to our recipe.So, when the whole cooking process takes place that's when we can experience those special ingredients and can learn some of the finest cooking tips which when applied in any interest areas of our life can change the taste of our life like never before.

Also, as one of my favorite inspirational personality and the world-famous Indian Chef Sanjeev Kapoor says –

Trying and not succeeding is better than not trying at all!

So, I completely agree with him as I do have the same mindset. Hence, going ahead with the same mindset I decided and attempted to convert one of my most favorite authentic dream recipes of life into reality to feed the world just like him with my special ingredients but in my own unique ways and to feed my soul in return to change the taste of my life and for every individual in the world who is passionate about something to achieve in any sphere of life by transforming their innerself.

Now, let's see how much you like or love my authentic real-life recipe called "Universal Power of Alphabetical Series" to get inspired and to try something new in your Life kitchen too to transform your 'SELF" into something meaningful.

Transform your SELF, to transform your LIFE to achieve true freedom or financial freedom in your own unique authentic ways because when you compare both words there is only one letter difference "S" and "I" that can make a huge difference in your LIFE too if you understand your – S - ELF deeply means your "I" inside you to be converted as "We" once you realize your true potentials.

The way one letter or word can change the whole meaning of our existence in this universe similarly, one life can change the existence of other life in this Universe to make difference in others life and can leave a universal impact wherever we are in this universe.

Please note that —

Personal Transformation is not an overnight journey, it may take sleepness days and nights to transform your authentic "SELF" into meaningful existence as "LIFE" to let us live our life with fullest enthusiasm always (Kanika Sinha)

So, let's take a look as in how we can know and understand ourself better to shape our life at its best.

CHAPTER – I

Self – Awareness - Know, Understand and Accept Your "Self"

If you truly want to be an achiever in all spheres of life than, I have an action exercise for you to do it at your end before you start shaping your life your way.

And, if you are ready than let's do some prior cooking arrangements before you cook the delicious authentic recipe of your life your way and to shape your - self in best way.

Please take a look at the below given picture depicting different stages of life to deeply analyze all stages of your life, to get the clarity of where you are standing right now, to set the right amount of expectation from yourself before you swim any size of the ocean and to live your life with fullest enthusiasm always to avoid "feeling of emptiness" at any future stages of your life -

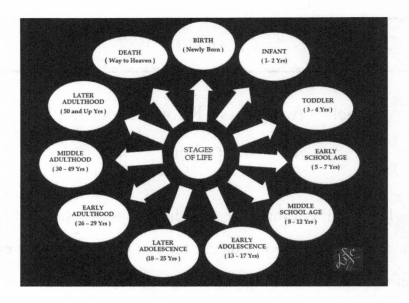

If we look at the life – cycle, we get so many opportunities from early school age to later adulthood stage to upgrade our thought process and to become better or best version then yesterday but, we can only do so if we realize the need deeply and once we realize, than, assuming each stage just like new day filled with new hopes and possibilities before departing for heaven, we should try to fill our and others life with heavenly experiences on this earth as much as we can in some meaningful ways.

So, which stage are you or your life is?

KANIKA SINHA

It's just the matter of understanding and accepting the facts the way they are thereafter the process of advancement becomes easygoing. Trust me!

We just have to be honest with ourselves as much as we can for overall growth and development and once you are done with the analysis, remember two things before starting your journey *"Age is just the number"* and *"Better late than never* "as I did to make all the difference in my life today with pure optimistic attitude.

As, I love asking questions to myself and my friends too, to have a two-way communication flow so, before I seek answers from you to my necessary questions, I have proactively given my answers to all the questions that I have for you so, you just need to answer honestly at your end and see how your own thought process is, so that, you can upgrade your mind with some relevant knowledge and can continue your efforts of putting your *Self* on the better life path then yesterday –

- *How do you define life?*
- *What would you like to do with the single blessed life?*
- *How would you like to do it?*

How do you define life?

When you live your dreams in reality with the fullest enthusiasm without any regret by being the best version of your true self and in line with the purpose of your soul on this earth because -

A meaningful life is not being rich, being popular, being highly educated, or being perfect. It is about being real, being humble, being able to share ourselves and touch the lives of others. It is only than that we could have a full, happy, and contended life.

What would you like to do with the single blessed life?

Would only uplift yourself because you deserve a better life or are you a compassionate and helpful soul who wants to inspire or serve others as well by setting up an example because you know and understand that "We rise by uplifting others".

How would you like to do it?

Through any life improvement course or any mentor or teacher that can help you to accomplish all your goals or dreams your way.

So, in order to achieve everything, you wish to have in your life, you will have to throw some light on your "SELF" believing -

No one is perfect in this world but we can certainly try to improve us if we know and understand us better.

And, how we can do so is by observing our ACTIONS so far?

START with writing one WORD that defines you, Start with writing one STATEMENT that defines you, Start by writing one PARAGRAPH that defines you, Start by writing one PAGE that defines you,

So that you know something about your good and bad self and can work on the gaps to be the better and best version of your SELF then you were yesterday by replacing one bad word with good word by performing some good actions adding value to your life.

To help you fill up the gaps if any, I have a very interesting yet cost effective method of self-learning and development i.e. to treat your BRAIN just like Wikipedia until you reach your final destination or accomplish any goals of your life every time you try something new because rock solid words do have the rocking power to break your mental limits and change your life forever. I bet!

So, Is your brain ready, to become one of the most powerful Wikipedia? If yes, than let me share the delicious ingredients or powerful words that I used to innovate my innerself or new version then yesterday to enjoy more versatile authentic flavors in my life being jack of all trades but master of none.... Ha – Ha to live my life with fullest enthusiasm always.

> *Powerful WORDS are just like solid WALL so,*
> *when you read and act, it passes strong optimistic*
> *vibes to your Mind, Heart and Soul!*

HAPPY READING for HAPPY ACTIONS to have HAPPY LIFE!

CHAPTER – II

Create unique dictionary of powerful words to work like authentic mentor or guide

A,B,C,D,E,F,G,H,I,J,K,L,M,N,O,P,Q,R,S,T,U,V,W,X,Y,Z

Words do have the power to change your life forever because they have the power to keep you firm and determined until you accomplish what you want to accomplish and helps you to improve your credibility to your highest self as an accountability partner responsible for your success unconditionally !

A,B,C,D,E,F,G,H,I,J,K,L,M,N,O,P,Q,R,S,T,U,V,W,X,Y,Z

In a nutshell, if we make use of the alphabetical series in more intelligent way, we can shape our life in much better way because the equation of life says -

Alphabets =>Words => Meanings => Actions => Results => Success = MEANINGFUL LIFE

So, if we keep our mind filled with some powerful words with powerful meaning than whenever we will act will always act powerfully and we wouldn't have to give up on something we genuinely love to live a meaningful life always.

Let's say, if we arrange twenty-six letters of the English alphabetical series more intelligently by creating our own dictionary of favorite words or ingredients because they can show us the way of living the life than how delicious would our dream life recipe be?

For Example –

A – Always B – Be C – Cool,

D – Don't have E – Ego with F – Friends and Family

G – Give up on H – Hurting I – Individuals,

J – Just K – Keep L – Loving M – Mankind,

N – Never O – Omit your P – Prayers

Q – Quietly R – Remember God,

S – Speak T – Truth,

U – Use V – Valid W – Words, and

X – Xpress Y – Your Z – Zeal!

Doesn't this series sounds so amazing and looks pretty much interesting?

If yes, than, what if we try teaching our next generation in a similar way as a teacher or parent or guide or mentor by asking them to practice the powerful enlisted words as much as they can by doing something that they genuinely like or love doing to help them shape their life from much early or middle school age and to help them create their own dictionary of more powerful words as a result of their own actions just the way I created after converting all my dreams into reality so far which I am sure will always help me just like my authentic mentor throughout my life as a source of guidance at any stage of life in this competitive world and would always help me to stretch my creativity skills at par.

Since, these words genuinely worked as my mentor, guide, teacher and helped me to reach where I am today so, before sharing the detailed list, my dear friend, I have a cooking tip for you –

Life is like a book where every new chapter has the beautiful side to it
Just keep turning the page with an optimistic mind !

And, to do so, just keep acting, reading and writing all the real chapters of your life somewhere until your life story becomes an inspirational source of education, empowerment, enlightenment, encouragement and entertainment in someone's life as a helping hand to help reduce sign of ageing from much early age.... Ha – Ha!

Now, let us look at the alphabetical series, to know, what are those powerful words or ingredients that we have been talking about as a method of self – education and has the power to change the taste of your life and increase the dimensions of life absolutely your own unique way.

Alphabetical Series –

A, B, C, D, E, F, G, H, I, J, K, L, M, N, O, P, Q, R, S, T, U, V, W, X, Y, Z

Alphabet - A

Words – Aptitude, Attitude, Altitude, Aggressive, Ambitious, Action, Ambivert, Adventurous, Accomplishment, Appreciate, Artist

Meaning of Words -

APTITUDE – A natural ability to do something or knowing your natural talent or interest

So, find out where your natural talent lies?

ATTITUDE – A settled way of positive thinking

ALTITUDE – Distance between the ground and the universe

It's not the APTITUDE, it's your ATTITUDE,
that will determine your ALTITUDE!

(Zig Ziglar)

AGGRESSIVE – Pursuing talent or interests passionately.

AMBITIOUS – Having or showing a strong desire and determination to succeed in any activity in motion.

Your level of ambition will define the level of intensity! (Kanika Sinha)

ACTION – Any activity in motion.

An old saying goes, *"Actions speak louder than words"* so just ACT.

AMBIVERT – Ambi means both extrovert and introvert.

"A balance of introversion and extroversion is the most powerful ambiversion of yourself"

Be an ambivert to live a balanced life.

ADVENTUROUS – Willing to take risk or to try out new methods, ideas, and experiences, full of excitement.

Life is an adventurous journey, explore your limits to live fearlessly ! (Kanika Sinha)

ACCOMPALISHMENT – Achievement of any goal or activity in motion.

Every small or big accomplishment begins with the decision to try(Unknown)

APPRECIATE – An ability to make someone feel good about their accomplishments because -

Appreciation is an act of kindness,

So, when appreciation happens, the person who gets appreciated feels good,

When the person feels good, productivity level goes up,

When productivity level goes up, self - value increases,

When the self - value increases, self - esteem increases,

When self – esteem increases, self- worth and credibility increases,

When self – worth and credibility increases, the level of personal peace increases and

When the level of personal peace increases, universal peace and growth happens at universal level! (Kanika Sinha)

Be Appreciative to set an inspirational example!

ARTISTS – Performer

Be the artist of your own life – Sketch your dream life, fill it with your choice of colors, blend all the colors to perfection with all your mind, heart and soul with patience until your product reflects your highest inner self (Kanika Sinha)

Alphabet - B

Words – Better, Best

Meaning of Words -

BETTER – Higher quality

BEST – Excellent quality

"If you have the option, choose the best; but if you don't have the option, than perform better to be the best" (Unknown)

"Good, better, best. Never let it rest until your good is better and your better is best"

(Unknown)

"Sometimes good and better things fall apart so that best things can fall into place "(Buddha)

Alphabet - C

Words – Commotion, Communication, Clarity, Choice, Connection, Confidence, Courage, Challenges, Compassionate, Competitive, Consistent, Commitment, Charismatic, Change, Contentment, Contribute, Character, Co – Operate, Celebration

Meaning of Words -

COMMOTION – A confused state of mind

COMMUNICATION – The process of expressing thoughts and feelings through some meaningful actions to have clear mindset.

For example – Expressing everything that comes to your mind and heart than sorting out to get the clarity to feed your soul.

Self – communication is the key to success! (Kanika Sinha)

CLARITY – The quality of being clear in your mind, heart and soul

CHOICE – Selected as one's favorite

Choice is the most powerful tool we have
Everything boils down to choice

We exist in a field of infinite possibilities

Every choice we make shuts an infinite number

of doors and opens an infinite number of doors.

At any point, we can change the direction of our

lives through a simple choice. It is all in our hands,

heart, mind, and soul.

CONNECTION – Staying connected with your true self.

CONFIDENCE – A feeling of self-assurance arising from ones own abilities or qualities.

> *Crying shatters your confidence*
> *Trying builds up your confidence*

Choice is yours!

Also,

> *Confidence on the outside begins by living with integrity on the inside (Brian Tracy)*

COURAGE – Brave, Bold, Fearless

> *Courage doesn't mean you don't get scared*
> *Courage means you don't let the fear stop you*

CHALLENGES – To compete with something difficult that requires great effort and determination.

When we limit our imaginations, we limit our challenges, and when we limit our challenges, we limit our growth!(Kanika Sinha)

"Don't limit your challenges, challenge your limits" (Shilpa Shetty).

The greatest challenge in life is discovering who you are,

The second greatest is being happy with what you find!

COMPASSIONATE – An ability to show concern for others wellbeing.

COMPETITIVE – Compete with your yesterday version to create your future version

CONSISTENT – Continuous efforts having stable optimistic approach towards life above any negative situations and circumstances

Slow and steady wins the race, if you put consistent efforts (Kanika Sinha)

COMMITTMENT – The state or quality of being dedicated to your purpose of life

CHARISMATIC – Compelling charm that inspires devotion in others resulting into a winning over life.

CHANGE – The act of becoming different or be the better or best version of yourself then yesterday

Be the change you wish to see in this world, to bring the change in the lives of your loved one!

(Kanika Sinha)

CONTENTMENT – Feeling of satisfaction

"If you are content with who you are right now, you are not aware who you could be if you were willing to strive" (Sadh guru)

CONTRIBUTE – Give in order to help achieve or provide something.

CHARACTER – The mental and moral qualities distinctive to an individual, True Nature or self.

CO – OPERATE – Work jointly towards the same goal.

Life becomes more beautiful when CONTRIBUTION and CO – OPERATION becomes much more important than healthy COMPETITION in anything you and your loved ones do.

CELEBRATION – The action of marking one's pleasure at an important event or occasion

Beautiful life should not only be lived, it should be celebrated, so celebrate all your wins whenever you can!

Alphabet – D

Words – Difficulty, Desire, Decision, Determination, Discipline, Devotion, Destination, Destiny

Meaning of Words -

DIFFICULTY – Anything which is difficult to understand and accomplish

Difficulties come into your life just not to shake you but to make more refined version of your true self (Kanika Sinha)

A negative thinker sees a difficulty in every opportunity, A positive thinker sees an opportunity in every difficulty.

Choice is yours!

DESIRE – A strong feeling of wanting to have something or to accomplish something

"When desire to succeed is greater than the fear of failure, miracle happens." (Unknown)

DECISION – The process or action of deciding to do something or fulfill your desires.

"Make a decision! If that doesn't work, make another and another and another. Keep doing until you break through" (Brian Tracy).

DETERMINATION – Firmness of achieving goals and purpose in life.

"You can find inspiration from others, but determination is solely your responsibility" (Dodinsky)

DISCIPLINE – To obey rules or a code of behavior by training your mind to stay progressive everyday

"Self – Discipline begins with the mastery of your thoughts. If you don't control what you think, you can't control what you do" (Unknown)

DEVOTION – Showing enthusiasm for any activity.
DESTINATION – Your ultimate stop or the end point.

Don't stop until you reach to the top" (Priyanka Chopra)
A difficult road often leads to beautiful destination so keep going (Zig Ziglar)

DESTINY – The hidden power believed to control what will happen in the future, fate.
So,

Difficulty brings changes,
Desire changes nothing,
Decision changes something,
Determination changes everything

You are just one decision away from a totally different life to change your destiny because

Destiny is not created by the shoes we wear but by the steps we take.

Alphabet - E

Words – Explore, Experiment, Experience, Enjoy, Evaluate, Educate, Enlighten, Energize, Empower, Express, Entertain

Meaning of Words -

EXPLORE – Travel in order to learn or familiarize oneself with any subject.

What is your favorite subject? Mine is LIFE!

EXPERIMENT – Examine, Analyze, Study, Test and Trial.

EXPERIENCE – Practical contact with and observation of facts or events in reality.

ENJOY – Taking delight or pleasure in any activity or project you are exploring,

experimenting, and experiencing.

EVALUATE – Assess the worth of work that you are exploring and enjoying.

EDUCATE – Absorb findings to learn and upgrade your mind with new refined knowledge.

ENLIGHTEN – Take greater knowledge and understanding of any subject.

Self – enlightenment is the key to success (Kanika Sinha)

The more you will practice all the words starting with "E" alphabet, the more you will enlighten yourself.

ENERGIZE – To pass on positive energies

"Everything is energy,
Your thoughts begin it,
Your emotions amplify it,
And your actions increase its momentum" (Unknown)

EMPOWER – Process of becoming powerful after learning something practically.

Empowerment comes through Education,
Education comes through Self – Education,
Self – Education comes through Self – Learning,
Self – Learning comes through Actions,

Actions comes through Thoughts and Thoughts comes through Actions and spiritual Belief – System!

EXPRESS – Express your complete satisfaction

ENTERTAIN – To spread positive vibes

"Explore and Experience your highest authentic self beyond imagination to entertain the universe around you "(Kanika Sinha)

Alphabet - F

Words – Forget, Freedom, Fearless, Focus, Flexibility, Failure

Meaning of Words -

FORGET – An easygoing ability to let go of something that you just like, to focus sharply on something that you love.

FREEDOM – The power or right to act, speak, or think as one wants without hindrance.

"Freedom lies in being bold" (Unknown)

FEARLESS – Audacious, Courageous

You will never know your limits until you become
fearless ! (Kanika Sinha)

How do you define fear?

Fear everything and run, or
Face everything and rise

Choice is yours!

FOCUS – An ability to concentrate on your goal. The center of interest or activity

Focus! Focus! Focus!

FLEXIBILITY – Willingness to change or modify

Be stubborn about your goals and flexible about
your methods to be your best version! (Kanika
Sinha)

FAILURE – The omission of expected or required actions

"Failure is not falling down but refusing to get up"
(Unknown)
You only fail when you stop trying! (Unknown)

Alphabet - G

Words – Genuine, Go-Getter, Goal, Generous, Goodness, Greatness

Meaning of Words -

GENUINE – Authentic, Real, Original, Sincere, Truthful

GO-GETTER – High achiever

GOAL – Purpose of achieving something.

> *"Anything not written is merely a desire not a goal "(Brian Tracy)*

How to define goal?

G – Greatest

O – Outstanding

A- Achievements of

L – Life

So, set a goal so big that you can't achieve it until you grow into the person who can!

> *Set Peace of mind as your highest goal and organize your life around it! (Brian Tracy)*

GENEROUS – Showing readiness to give more of something as money or time than is strictly necessary or expected.

Be generous enough with yourself, to be generous enough with the people around you!

GOODNESS – Integrity, Honesty, the quality or state of being good

To raise the level of goodness, the scale of goodness should also be equally good! (Kanika Sinha)

GREATNESS – The quality of being distinguished

Doing easy thing is good, but doing something right is truly great! (Kanika Sinha)
You don't have to be great at something to start, but you have to start to be great at something! (Zig Ziglar)

Alphabet - H
Words – Hard work, Honest, Humble, Habit, Hopeful, Humanity, Happy

Meaning of Words -

HARDWORK – Diligent, Painstaking

Work hard, Have fun, Make history with victory!
(Kanika Sinha)
What comes easy won't last long, and what lasts
long won't come easy! (Unknown)

HONEST – Sincere with yourself

HUMBLE – Having or showing a modest or low estimate of one's own importance.

HABIT – A regular tendency or practice especially the one that is hard to give up

"Successful people are simply those with successful
habits" (Brian Tracy)

How to define habit?

H – Healthy

A – Actions make you

B – Better or Best

I – In

T – Time

It takes twenty-one days to make or break good habit for building a happy life tomorrow.

HOPEFUL – Feeling optimistic and confident about future events to happen.

HUMANITY – The fact or condition of being human.

> *Humanity is the only purest religion because that gives an opportunity to connect with the world around with an open – mind, heart and soul! (Kanika Sinha)*

HAPPY – Feeling or expressing pleasure after achieving something what you want.

> *Happiness is a choice as a result of some decision. Nothing will make you happy until you choose to be happy. No person will make you happy unless you decide to be happy. Your happiness will not come to you. It can only come from you!*

And, when you pace up or start gaining the momentum through your actions in something that you truly love, you will experience and learn some more powerful words like -

Alphabet - I

Words – Intuitive, Intelligent, Imaginative, Intensity, Independence, Intellectual, Interdependence, Irreplaceable, Inspirational

Meaning of Words -

INTUITIVE – Using facts based on what one feels to be true even without conscious reasoning, strong ability to identify strong feeling of conviction.

INTELLIGENT – Having high mental capacity to understand the high-level side of any particular subject.

IMAGINATIVE – An ability to think or dream as high as possible.

Push your imaginative skills as high as possible to
fly just like an eagle! (Kanika Sinha)

INTENSITY – The quality of being intense to improve your version.

INDEPENDENCE – Ability to operate strongly and single-handedly.

INTELLECTUAL – Having high level understanding powers to see the positive side of any situation in life.

INTERDEPENDENCE – The dependence of two or more people on each other

Try to be independent by supporting yourself so much that others can feel supportive and dependent on you anytime,

Try encouraging and practicing inter dependence so much that you can achieve the true level of freedom anytime,

The concept of interdependence boosts an independent spirit so much that each person can live life freely and happily without feeling suppressed or dominated at any time, so if we practice independence and interdependence, the strategy for living a balanced, peaceful, and content life will become the way of living the life!

(Kanika Sinha)

IRREPLACEABLE – Unique, Incomparable, One -of-a -kind

Be the one!

INSPIRATIONAL – Making you feel full of hope or encouragements, motivational.

Who or what Inspires you?

Find out with whom you share the same level of interest or who is already on the same journey as you are, to always stay motivated by thinking "If they can do, I can do it too"

Also, if you are an ardent learner, you can learn so much from the natural sources of inspiration in the universe we live in as they always try to teach us some important lessons in life to help us stay firm, towards the purpose of our life so another best way to win over life is to -

Adopt the pace of nature because her secret is patience! (Ralph Waldo Emerson)

So, pick up what inspires you most and keep moving towards the direction you want to move –

MOUNTAINS says -

Hikers walk over me, but I still choose to be silent because I give them confidence to keep moving in the direction they want to travel.

OCEAN says -

I help swimmers to convert their ordinary strength into extra – ordinary strength by allowing them to swim and reach to the ground surface or crossing the ocean.

FLOWERS says -

Likers pluck me, but I still choose to let the plucker do it again because I feel happy to see happy faces.

SUN says -

I stand alone but still choose to shine and spread positive energies around.

MOON says -

I stand alone but I still choose to spread light during the darkest hours of the day.

STARS says -

We believe that unity is integrity and we can spread more powerful light during darkest hours of someone's life.

TREES says -

We choose to stay firm in our roots even if we have been declared dead during the fall.

We don't talk about trees getting older
We say they are "GROWING"
Let's use the same term for ourselves because

We're not getting older, we are just growing

That's the spirit of living an authentic life with fullest enthusiasm!

Alphabet - J

Words – Joy, Jealous, Jack of all trades but master of none

Meaning of Words -

JOY – A feeling of great pleasure and happiness in doing something that you love

The *joy of giving* is one of the greatest joys one can experience by offering what they have as much as possible to create endless enduring moments in others lives and making their lives more meaningful and worthwhile !

> *Doing good for others is not a duty, it's a joy, as it increases your own health and happiness!*

JEALOUS – Feeling or showing envy of someone of their achievements

> *Jealousness makes you bitter,*
> *Competitiveness makes you better*

Choice is yours!

JACK- OF –ALL-TRADES but master of none. So, why not try becoming the master of something that you love doing the most to live all your minor and major dreams into reality.

Do everything you love to do, to enjoy versatile flavors as much as you can, to explore the size and depth of an artistic ocean inside you so much so that, that it makes you super creative in anything you love doing the most!

Alphabet - K

Words – Knowledge, Kindness

Meanings of Words -

KNOWLEDGE – Facts, Information, and Skills acquired by a person through experience or education, the theoretical or practical understanding of a subject.

Knowledge is a lifetime, permanent and non – materialistic asset that will always give you higher returns more than any materialistic assets in your life! (Kanika Sinha)

KINDNESS - The quality of being generous

Be kind to yourself and others! (Kanika Sinha)

Alphabet - L

Words – Listen, Love, Lead, Live, Laugh, Life, Legend

Meaning of Words –

LISTEN – Hearing your own inner voice.

Listening Voices doesn't mean, one should stop listening to their own VOICE! (Kanika Sinha)

LOVE – An intense feeling of deep affection, fondness for something

How to define LOVE?

L – Learn

O – Our

V – Value

E – Every day

Deepest love with life happens when your mind, heart, and soul are in line with each other so, increase and learn your value with each passing day with everything you love doing because the secret of success is found in daily life and than refine your version gradually to be your best self.

LEAD – Be in charge and take command of your own life.

Before you lead others, lead yourself first with something you love! (Kanika Sinha)

LIVE – Remain alive or active

Do something that keeps you alive or active until you start living super active life with something that you would love to do the most everyday! (Kanika Sinha)

Don't ask yourself what the world needs, ask yourself what makes you come alive and than, go and do that. Because what the world needs is people who have come alive!

(Howard Washington Thurman)

LAUGH – A source of fun

Life laughs at you when you are unhappy,
Life smiles at you when you are happy,

But life salutes you when you make others happy
(Charlie Chaplin)

LIFE – Living a meaningful life in line with the purpose of your soul

Life is a onetime offer. Use it well!

LEGEND – Popular personality

Love, lead, live, and laugh genuinely to live your
life with fullest enthusiasm like a legend!
(Kanika Sinha)
Small needs gives rise to bigger NEEDS,
Bigger needs gives rise to bigger DREAMS,
Bigger dreams gives rise to bigger ACTIONS,
Bigger actions gives rise to bigger COURAGE and
Bigger courage gives rise to biggest LEGENDS!
(Kanika Sinha)

Alphabet - M

Words – Mistake, Moral, Measure, Money, Minimalist

Meaning of Words -

MISTAKE – Errors, trials while attempting something

A person who never tried anything new, never made a mistake (Albert Einstein)

A life spent making mistakes is not only more honorable but more useful than a life spent doing nothing (George Bernard Shaw)

MORAL – Concerned with the principles of right and wrong behavior, high minded, honorable, noble, clean living, holding, or manifesting high principles for proper conduct

MEASURE - Quantify, Evaluate, Assess one's actions carefully

MONEY – The assets, property, and resources owned by someone or something

Money satisfies the feeling of hunger temporarily, but education satisfies the feeling of hunger permanently! (Kanika Sinha)

MINIMALISTS - A person who advocates or practices minimalism in any form of art to achieve maximum results

A minimalist prefers the minimal amount or degree of something. In art history, the minimalists were artists whose work involved extremely simple gestures and ideas. The art they created is also referred to as minimalist.

Be the one who produces maximum results with minimum resources to maximize your very own minimum potentials.

> *What is your Minimum and Maximum potential?*
> *Minimum Potential – The abilities that you have.*
> *Maximum Potential – How and to what extent you can convert your wasteland into wonderland using those abilities to maximize your self – worth and credibility.*

Alphabet - N

Words – No, Never Give up

Meaning of Words –

NO - Next Opportunity or New Opportunity so never give up!

> *Give up, give in, or give it all you have got (Unknown)*

And,

> *With sunset today is gone,*

With sunrise another today will come,

So just the way, sun sets and rises again,

Keep rising every single day with never-give-up

attitude! (Kanika Sinha)

Alphabet - O

Words – Opportunists, Outstanding, Overthinking, Out of the box, Ownership

Meaning of Words -

OPPORTUNISTS – Someone who tries to get an advantage or something valuable from a situation to make the most out of time

OUTSTANDING - Exceptionally good, superb

OVERTHINKING – Thinking about the problems that doesn't even exist

OUT OF THE BOX – Thinking and doing ordinary things in an extraordinary way

OWNERSHIP – Owning your Thoughts and doing Actions accordingly

Alphabet - P

Words – Pain, Purification, Passion, Purpose, Priority, Planning, Pace, Patience, Positivity, Permanence, Perseverance, Progression, Perfection, Peace, Power, Performance, Possible, Procrastination, Pray

Meaning of Words -

PAIN – Any mental, emotional, and physical suffering or challenge

The best way to define is?

P – Positive

A – Actions

I – In

N – Negative

S – Situations

As long as you feel pain, you are still alive,
As long as you make mistakes, you are still human,
And as long as you keep trying there is still hope,
(Susan gale)

PURIFICATION - The process of purifying the inner self

Practice all words starting with alphabet *"E"* in systematic order by doing something that you either like or love doing and you are all set to purify your inner self

PASSION – Strong and barely controllable emotions, a very powerful feeling, fondness, enthusiasm or desire for anything.

> *Working hard for something we don't care about is*
> *called stress. Working hard for something we love*
> *is called "passion" (Simon Sinek)*

PURPOSE – The reason for which something needs to be done, the aim or intention of doing something.

> *People with purpose, goals, and visions have no time*
> *for drama. They invest their energy in creativity*
> *and focus on living a positive life (Unknown)*

PRIORITY – The order of importance

> *To change your life, you need to define or re- define*
> *your priorities! (Kanika Sinha)*

PLANNING – The process of making action plan for achieving goals

PACE – A single step taken when walking or running consistently at a continuous speed towards achieving your plans because one step does makes a huge difference in your life.

PATIENCE – The capacity to accept or tolerate delay or the ability to wait for something to happen with optimistic attitude.

> *Patience is not about the ability to wait, but is an ability to keep a good attitude while waiting too! (Unknown)*
>
> *The person who is a master of patience is a master of everything! (Unknown)*

POSITIVITY – An optimistic outlook towards something to happen.

> *"If you have the spirit of understanding everything in a positive way, you will enjoy each and every moment of life whether it's a pressure or a pleasure." (Unknown)*

"Your mind is a magnet

If you think of blessings, you attract blessings and

If you think of problems, you attract problems

Always cultivate good thoughts

Always remain optimistic"

PERMANENCE – Stability in thoughts and actions

Keep going until your positive thoughts show sign of stability! (Kanika Sinha)

There is nothing so stable as change! (Kanika Sinha)

PERSEVERANCE – Steadfastness in doing something despite difficulty or delay in achieving success.

PROGRESSION – The process of developing or moving gradually towards a more advanced state, series of actions or trials while working on something since long.

When you are obsessed about uplifting others along with self-development, the progression process becomes more satisfying! (Kanika Sinha)

Progression is more important than Perfection if we understand different stages of progression to progress with peace of mind -

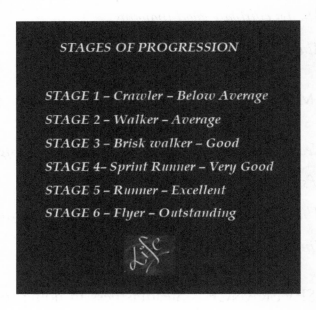

STAGES OF PROGRESSION

STAGE 1 – Crawler – Below Average

STAGE 2 – Walker – Average

STAGE 3 – Brisk walker – Good

STAGE 4– Sprint Runner – Very Good

STAGE 5 – Runner – Excellent

STAGE 6 – Flyer – Outstanding

So, just keep moving even if you are crawling because, sometimes, the smallest step in the right direction ends up being the biggest step of your life. Tiptoe if you must, but keep moving to experience all stages of progression and to become the perfectionists in your deepest interest areas of life .

PERFECTION – The condition, state, or quality of being free from all flaws and defects.

KANIKA SINHA

It's not about being perfect. It's about an effort and when you bring that effort every single day to your work, that's where the transformation happens and that's how the change occurs in a perfect way at perfect time.

Practice makes the man perfect!

PEACE – A quiet and calm state of mind after achieving intended purpose.

Mind at peace makes you shine like a noble solid golden piece! (Kanika Sinha)
Set peace of mind as your highest goal and organize your life around it (Brian Tracy)

POWER - Having great power or strength

You need power only when you want to do something harmful otherwise love is enough to make everything happen (Charlie Chaplin)

PERFORMANCE – The action or process of carrying out any activity or project in the way it was meant to be delivered.

POSSIBLE – When an impossible task becomes possible

"Everything becomes possible, but the impossible takes little longer because great things take time"
(Unknown)

PROCRASTINATION – The action of delaying or postponing something especially that requires immediate attention.

Immediate actions are the key to success and procrastination is the key to failure! (Kanika Sinha)

PRAY – Worship God

Prayer is the key of the morning and the bolt of the evening so start and end your day with prayer!

Alphabet - Q

Words – Question, Quantity, Quality

Meaning of Words -

QUESTION – A question is not who is going to let me, it's who is going to stop me.

Repeatedly ask yourself below questions throughout your journey

Where are you?

What you can do more?

Where do you want to be?

QUANTITY – Excessive volume of something unnecessary that needs to be reduced or removed completely.

QUALITY – A high level of value or excellence

Quality is the result of quantity! (Kanika Sinha)

Alphabet - R

Words – Resilience, Responsible, Reliable, Resourceful, Respectful, Roots, Rebellious, Reinvent

Meaning of Words-

RESILIENCE – An ability to recover fast from setback.

RESPONSIBLE – Having control over your life and taking care of yourself.

RELIABLE – Trustworthy, Dependable

RESOURCEFUL – Being able to perform multiple task

RESPECTFUL – Well-mannered, worthy of deserving respect

ROOTS – The place of origination

Stay connected with your roots to keep yourself firm and determined towards your goal!

REBELLIOUS – Showing desire to resist authority or control for matters what you believe is right.

REINVENT –Taking up a very different job or way of life

Cross all stages of progression to reinvent your true self! (Kanika Sinha)

Alphabet - S

Words – Solidify, Smart, Smile, Straightforward, Spiritual, Systematic, Simplicity, Strength, Stability, Standard of living and giving, Self, Selfless, Selfish Self-starter, Self-Motivated, Self-analysis, Stubborn, Success, Sweat, Spontaneity

Meaning of Words –

SOLIDIFY – Become solid version of yourself through contentment.

SMART – Finding quick resolutions to any kind of obstacles.

SMILE – Cheerfulness

How to define Smile?

S – See, M – Miracle, I – In, L – life, E – Everyday!

Travel unlimited miles with smile on your face to make your journey easygoing! (Kanika Sinha)

STRAIGHTFORWARD – Honest, frank, simple, easy to understand and up front.

Simple and Straightforward approach towards life helps in shaping your own and others life! (Kanika Sinha)

SPIRITUAL – Religious, sacred and divine, relating to deep feelings and beliefs

Are you spiritually inclined towards something because you believe in having deepest soul satisfaction?

SYSTEMATIC – Acting according to a fixed plan or system in efficient, orderly, organized way.

SIMPLICITY – The quality or condition of being easy to understand.

"Simplicity is the ultimate sophistication means simple isn't banal—it's elegant." (Unknown)

STRENGTH – Having powers to move or perform any given task.

It's important to do whats best for you, whether people approve of it or not
This is your life. You know whats good for you and remember, Self – Love takes strength
(Unknown)

STABILITY – The state of being stable, firm, steadiness, strength, balance of mind, heart, and soul.

STANDARD OF LIVING and GIVING – Raise your self-worth to raise your giving standards not just your living standards

"If you rise, you raise your standards and as you raise your standards, you rise."(Unknown)

SELF – A person's essential being that distinguishes them from others by knowing everything about their self means all strengths, weaknesses, opportunities and threats.

SELFLESS – Finding happiness in doing good for other people more than one's own happiness

SELF-CENTERED – Concerned about self for creating WIN – WIN situations.

Making yourself a priority is not a selfish act, its necessary to make your victory viable !

SELF-STARTER – A person who is sufficiently motivated or ambitious to start a new business or to pursue further education without the help of others.

SELF-MOTIVATED – Motivated to do or achieve something because of one's own enthusiasm or interest without needing pressure from others.

Self-Starters and Self - Motivated people have a better edge than those who wait for encouragements and boosters from others, super-energized people should not waste their precious time in looking for approvals. They should simply keep moving to

become an energy booster for other people around them.

SELF-ANALYSIS – The person who believes in doing deep analysis about self.

STUBBORN – Headstrong, Willful, Strong – Willed

Stubbornness gives winning edge on everything you wish to have in your life provided, if you have positive intentions! (Kanika Sinha)

SUCCESS – Accomplishment of any goal

The elevator to success is out of order. You will have to use the stairs, one step at a time (Joe Girard)
Success consists of going from failure to failure without loss of enthusiasm" - (Winston Churchill)
Success is the sum of small efforts repeated day in and day out (Unknown)

SWEAT – Wetness

Are you sweating to fuel your passion every day?

SPONTANEITY – An act or quality of acting without thinking in advance

Sometimes spontaneous roller coaster drive really works well than planning because planning always gives you heads - up and instill an amount of fear inside you and can stop you from giving your bests! Be fierce and Stay strong to experience the real joy and adventures of life with an Extra - Ordinary strength and courageous attitude! (Kanika Sinha)

Alphabet - T

Words – Travel, Truthful, Trustworthy, Thinker, Temporary, Test and Try, Time

Meaning of Words -

TRAVEL – Moving from one place to another

Travel as much as you can,
As long as you can,
As far as you can so that, you can see further and
Continue your journey until you reach your highest self because
Life is not meant to be at one place if you want to explore your best self!

TRUTHFUL – Being honest with yourself and others.

TRUSTWORTHY – Able to be relied on as reliable, Dependable

THINKER – A person who thinks deeply and seriously.

"Your life is a reflection of your thoughts. Think well" (Danielle Pierre)

TEMPORARY – Lasting for only a limited period of time, not permanent in nature.

"Temporary failures are better than permanent failures " (Unknown)

Every situation in life is temporary. So, when life is good, make sure you enjoy and receive it fully and when life is not so good, remember that it will not last forever because better days are on the way.

Now, my most favorite word that gave me universal powers to re – define, re- invent and innovate the better self that I am today is -

TRY – Make an effort or attempt to do something new or different

How to define TRY?

T – Take Action

R – Repeat Action and

Y – See YOUR new version

So,

> **TRY EVERYTHING !**
>
> *Try Everything what you love doing .....*
>
> *To explore your maximum potentials by diving into your own artistic sea*
> *To discover the life path you are meant to travel with greatest zeal*
> *To find out and create everything what you love doing the most*
> *To create your unique self and to love yourself the most*
> *To make new mistakes and to learn everyday*
> *To apply learnings and grow your self everyday*
> *To achieve highest level of your highest self*
> *To have more reasons to fall in love with yourself*
> *To learn to get up and never give up on yourself*
> *To find your true and bestest friends within yourself*
> *To raise your Self – Worth and Credibility in the eyes of your own self*
> *To spiritualize and find the universe within yourself*
> *To create and live your dream life with fullest enthusiasm through Passion,*
> *Purpose, Patience, Permanence and Perseverance with deepest desire*
> *To create the world you truly desire and*
> *To set the universal stage on fire !*

Don't worry about the failures, worry about the

chances you miss when you don't even try

(Jack Canfield)

Continually push yourself out of your comfort zone.

Push yourself to stretch your mind as you try new

things each day - (Brian Tracy)

And,

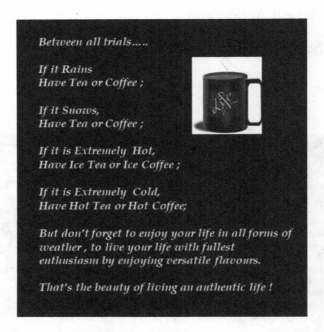

Between all trials.....

If it Rains
Have Tea or Coffee ;

If it Snows,
Have Tea or Coffee ;

If it is Extremely Hot,
Have Ice Tea or Ice Coffee ;

If it is Extremely Cold,
Have Hot Tea or Hot Coffee;

But don't forget to enjoy your life in all forms of
weather , to live your life with fullest
enthusiasm by enjoying versatile flavours.

That's the beauty of living an authentic life !

So, raise your energy levels as much as you can to raise the momentum passionately.

TIME – The moment you are living in or you want to live

How to define time?

T – Take

I – It

M – More

E – Enthusiastically

Because,

KANIKA SINHA

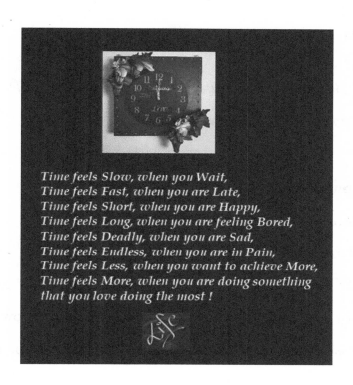

Time feels Slow, when you Wait,
Time feels Fast, when you are Late,
Time feels Short, when you are Happy,
Time feels Long, when you are feeling Bored,
Time feels Deadly, when you are Sad,
Time feels Endless, when you are in Pain,
Time feels Less, when you want to achieve More,
Time feels More, when you are doing something
that you love doing the most !

Every time, time is determined by your feelings and your psychological conditions, not by a clock.

So, enjoy every moment of your life by doing something that you love doing the most to make use of the time in the best possible way because time is more valuable than money, as you can get more money but you cannot get more time and if you do so money will follow you effortlessly.

> *Until you value yourself, you won't value your time. Until you value your time, you will not do anything with it (M. Scott Peck)*

THANKFUL – Filled with gratitude

Be thankful and grateful for everything in your life today and every day!

Alphabet - U

Words – Understand, Useful, Ultimate

Meaning of Words –

UNDERSTAND – Ability to understand your current stage of life and making efforts to improve your own life progressively for improving others life too as a mentor, guide and source of inspiration.

USEFUL – Beneficial, giving, or ready to give help

ULTIMATE – The best achievable or imaginable version of yourself.

Become the ultimate version of yourself to make your own life useful for others! (Kanika Sinha)

Alphabet - V

Words – Visualize, Version, Victorious

Meaning of Words -

VISUALIZE – Imagine your best self

"Imagine, create, share, and inspire to stay motivated (Kanika Sinha)

VERSION – Something different in certain respects from an earlier form.

VICTORIOUS – Successful, Conquering

Success is Never Permanent,
Failure is never final,
So, never stop trying until your victory makes a history!
"Visualize your best version, create it, and be victorious" (Kanika Sinha)

Alphabet - W

Words – Worry, Warrior, Work,

Meaning of Words -

WORRY – The act of worrying or the condition of being worried

Don't worry, just be happy by working towards your goals! (Kanika Sinha)

WARRIOR – A brave or experienced soldier or fighter

Try to be the warrior, not the worrier to win over

life in an optimistic way! (Kanika Sinha)

Worrying doesn't solve tomorrow's trouble, it takes

away today's peace so,

don't worry for anything and keep your life moving

with "SMILE"!

WORK – Any activity involving mental or physical efforts in order to achieve a purpose or result as a means of earning income or source of income to become financially free for life. So,

Work until your mind, heart, and soul connects

deeply and you start leaving your mark wherever

you travel in this world! (Kanika Sinha)

Alphabet - X

Words – X - Factor

Meaning of Word – X – Factor

X - FACTOR – A noteworthy special talent or quality that can take you to the top and can set you apart from rest of the world to help you become your better or best version then yesterday.

> *Hardships often prepare ordinary people for an extraordinary destiny (C.S LEWIS)*
> *"Even if you have an ordinary talent, with your hard work and patience you can always convert any ordinary talent into an extra – ordinary talent "(Kanika Sinha)*

Because,

> *We don't have to be extra-ordinary to live an extra – ordinary life,*
> *We just have to do little extra every day to live an ordinary life like an extra – ordinary!*

So, keep doing something extra everyday to build that X- factor through your hard work and patience to create an extra – ordinary life that you wish to live forever.

Alphabet - Y

Words – You

Meaning of Words -

YOU – Your true or highest self

"No one will know you, until you know your "self"
(Kanika Sinha)

Alphabet - Z

Words – Zest

Meaning of Words -

ZEST – Great energy or enthusiasm in pursuit of a cause or an objective to create best life for yourself.

So,

Live your life with the spirit as if, you will never get another opportunity to live your life your way,

Live your life with the spirit as if, this is the last opportunity that will never ever come your way,

Live your life with so much of passion and vigor in you as if, no one is more passionate than you,

Live your life with so much of self – respect as if ,you want to create the world who would love and honor you,

Live your life with all your heart as if, you will always be content within you,

Live your life to your fullest as if, you can still digest the zest in you !

Hope you liked my world of dictionary as I believe, it should help you and your loved ones too to shape rest of your life in a much better way by pushing your mind more than its original limit and to let you live your life with your fullest potentials always.

So, STRETCH your mind more on something you LOVE but, STRESS your mind less on something you just LIKE (Kanika Sinha)

Since, you always have the scope of advancement in whatever you do in your life provided you should get some form of mentorship in some form at any stage of your life so, when you do get the guidance or mentorship you should try adding some more powerful words in your own world of dictionary to act as powerful guide and to do that, keep on executing the knowledge that you have gained through this book as much as you can to be at your best self, to convert all your dreams into reality, to change the taste, improve the quality and increase the dimensions of your life to achieve your best self.

And, when you consistently make efforts to achieve any general purpose or goal or wish or dream in your life using authentic power of alphabetical series to help you fulfill all your needs or dreams than, you can discover your highest purpose of life too, to create and live a meaningful life ahead and to always come out as a performer and winner in every phase of your life if you have a winning and optimistic mindset.

Sounds exciting? Yeah, I could imagine so, what are we waiting for let's keep going buddy to help you find your authentic WHY and to help you transform your - self into something meaningful irrespective of any age and stage of life you are in right now believing-

> *Live and Let live is the best life policy to sustain*
> *personal peace and to spread universal peace!*
> *(Kanika Sinha)*

And, before you start converting all your dreams into reality, may I request you to play either your favorite music or my favorite music that relaxes your mind, heart and soul through the given link below on your laptop or mobile and close eyes for 3 - 4 mins to relax and calm your mind before you experience the magical transformation of your *"self"*.

https://www.youtube.com/watch?v=TRIsgsZfZL4 &feature=youtu.be

If you loved the music than, I highly recommend to continue listening the music until you finish reading this book for heavenly experiences in your life.

So, are you ready to innovate or reinvent your new self? and if yes, than let's start with defining your intent or purpose of your actions that you wish to achieve in your life to experience next level growth and success of your authentic self.

CHAPTER – III

Self – Regulation - Define purpose of actions to invest time on yourself wisely

Anything short following your dreams and passion is settling for mediocrity in life.

If the universe opens a door for you to follow a passion than, run through that door to convert all your dreams into reality before it closes and never opens again so,

> *What are the ingredients of a delicious recipe called DREAMS ?*
>
> *D – DETERMINATION*
> *R – RESULTS*
> *E – ENERGY*
> *A – ACTIONS*
> *M – MOMENTUM*
> *S – SUCCESS*
>
> *When you have the DETERMINATION to achieve your purpose, you deliver RESULTS ,*
> *When you deliver RESULTS, you raise your ENERGY ,*
> *When you raise your ENERGY , you perform more ACTIONS,*
> *When you perform more ACTIONS, you start gaining the MOMENTUM and*
> *When you start gaining the MOMENTUM, you rise above the ground to fly because the SUCCESS that you will experience through your own actions will not only be felt by the outside world but most importantly will be felt by your true authentic self .*
>
> *So, keep raising your self - worth and credibility progressively with each passing day with anything or everything you love doing to become the best version of your SELF, to convert all your dreams into reality, to change the taste, quality and dimensions of your life, to inspire people at large and to live your life with the fullest enthusiasm always through passion, purpose , patience, hard work and perseverance !*

And, to live your life with fullest enthusiasm, are you ready to learn and grow into the kind of version beyond your own imaginations above any challenges and limitations of your life?

If yes, than —

Let's begin my favourite talk show, by asking you some more questions-

-   Are you fed up and is experiencing boredom in your 9 to 5 job routine because you don't love what you do and is simply doing because you like doing it as you are shouldered with financial responsibilities to fulfill your basic set of needs of life? or

-   Are you wanting to take up a different way of life to enjoy life in a better way then yesterday because you are a dreamer and is seriously wanting to create your new best version to fulfill all your dreams your way as your own life boss giving you greater amount of flexibility for best work — life balance? or

-   Are you a beautiful soul working as a priceless homemaker and peacemaker and is willing to travel extra miles to add more feathers to your million-dollar achievers cap because – *Not every beauty king or queen wear crown. Some wear caps and serve as heroes or super heroes* to raise your self - worth and credibility as an Individual too by creating more powerful self – identity? or

- Does your kids need right amount of guidance at the right time for proper growth and development as you want to guide them with right set of knowledge to pace up with the competitive world by helping them to live a meaningful life from much early or middle school age? or

- Are you looking to completely innovate or invent more powerful version of your authentic self as a whole then you were yesterday by raising the level of happiness and contentment through self-learning and development process? or

- Are you experiencing any feeling of emptiness inside you and need helping hand to fill that empty space in your life to uplift your mind, heart and soul? or

- Are you feeling stuck at any stage of your life and need someone who can push your mind, heart and soul? or

- Are you experiencing any obstacles in any areas of your life and is looking for solutions to keep yourself moving? or

- Are you passionate about freedom or financial freedom by converting all your dreams into reality?

If the answer is YES again, to all the above questions than this book is for you and to help you resolve all your worries, let me give you a classic example from our daily routine because, I personally think that cooking is an interesting ART which 90 % of the world population does for xyz reasons on everyday basis and since it consumes lot of time, energy, money and hope so it actually pushes your creativity level towards your highest self in some authentic ways and helps you to acquire wisdom that can be applied in any sphere of your life therefore,

The one who can passionately, patiently and happily cook the delicious authentic food recipes in everyday life for themselves or for their near and dear ones can, also maximize his or her minimum potentials passionately, patiently and happily to an extent of becoming financially free without losing any enthusiasm if he or she has the strongest will power or desire to do so because, somewhere there already exist PASSION and we just need to push it more to become the next best version of our authentic self because to every current or original highest level there exist next higher or highest level and until we do something to move our mind, heart and soul we would never be able to explore our maximum limits or potentials of our authentic self.

So, when we do something on everyday basis consistently, it's quite natural that the intensity of our taste should also increases up with each passing day in some ways hence, I highly recommend, one should try to convert their passion into some kind of profession to raise their self – worth and credibility more to continue enjoying versatile flavors of life in an extra – ordinary authentic way.

Having said that, if we are an ardent foodie and wants to enjoy versatile authentic flavors in everyday life, wants to feed our loved ones means our family, friends and society with fresh optimistic energies to beat the challenges of their daily life and wants to live healthy and wealthy life at its best than -

Becoming a Home Chef to feed the mind, heart and soul of family and friends could be a passionate need or dream for someone to enjoy an ordinary life in an extraordinary authentic way but

Becoming the World Class Chef or Opening Restaurant or doing both to feed the mind, heart and soul of friends, family and world at large scale could be a passionate need or dream for someone and can be a different way of life to enjoy ordinary life in an extra – ordinary authentic way because,

Living an ordinary life in an extra – ordinary way or living an ordinary life in an ordinary way is absolutely the matter of choice of an individual once he or she gets deepest understanding about his or her authentic self.

And, to do so or to decide which way to choose, one must test their creative abilities or limits thoroughly and passionately by exploring, experimenting, experiencing, enjoying, evaluating, educating, enlightening, energizing, empowering, expressing and entertaining themselves on everyday basis to taste versatile flavors and innovate the new best version of his or her *"Authentic Self"* so-

Do what you can do, to know upto what extent you can do and

To know what you can do, and to what extent, EXPLORE the power of your authentic self passionately! (Kanika Sinha)

And, when you apply the same logic to any other interest areas of your life than, let me tell you, that you and your life will never be the same again, as you will just not fall in love with your new *self* but will also fall in love with the new bright colors of your life which you will get to see while on an authentic journey ahead by making difference in your own life and others life all your own unique way to make a perfect living.

So, to help you with all the information that you and your loved ones would need to innovate or invent the best version either as a Home Chef or World Class Chef or any other powerful version you wish to be as per your interest areas and to live your dream life your way let's get started with all the much needed cooking or reading fun to help you change the taste and dimensions of your life forever because your-

Level of Interest defines the Level of Intensity! (Kanika Sinha)

And, when your level of intensity paces up with time, that's when you are in the process of becoming the best version of your authentic self because somewhere deep down the heart and soul you have already started living your passion and purpose of your existence on this earth in some way and you are already on the journey of discovering the highest purpose of your life to live a more meaningful life ahead provided, if you pay little more attention to your inner voice.

So, please consider every single word of this book as an *Ingredient* and each motivational quote as the *Cooking Tip* to help you prepare the best version of your authentic self and to create the most delicious dream recipe of your life just the way I converted three of my dream recipes into reality for lifetime from my very own *"Lifekitchen"* using my favorite set of special ingredients D, R, E, A, M and S as depicted in the below picture -

AUTHENTIC REAL RECIPE OF MY LIFE

VINTAGE WALL CLOCK

KANIKA SINHA

To express my thoughts of valuing TIME and the authentic book that you are reading now all the way from my aromatic kitchen. Ha – Ha!

I literally have my standing desk inside my kitchen.

As, I enjoyed the taste or flavors of all the above authentic ingredients, I continued to make more use of it along with other set of powerful words or ingredients or spices or herbs consistently to stay progressive like –

DREAM, CREATE, ACHIEVE, SHARE, INSPIRE, PROGRESS and created many more other authentic real recipes for lifetime in every interesting areas of my life I was fond of to enjoy versatile flavors of life as a passionate artist and as a result I learnt the cooking tip -

> *You can do anything but, should definitely do something that covers every corner of your heart to satisfy your soul deeply if ART rules your heART!*
> *(Kanika Sinha)*

So, explore your maximum potentials passionately with your minimum potentials in any or every interest areas of your life that you simply love by using all authentic ingredients as mentioned above or by referring the dictionary of powerful words as shared in section no – II or by creating your own world of dictionary having your own favorite words to discover your true passion and highest purpose of life, to innovate the best version of your unique authentic self, to start the new journey towards creating your dream life with your new best version and to subsequently raise the level of happiness and contentment of your life then yesterday.

While, I was on the voyage of innovating my new self or doing self – enlightenment, here is my favorite poem written for you after going through with all of my authentic experiences -

With any form of ART, you will discover your eternal STRENGHTS,

With any form of ART, you will discover your eternal WEAKNESSES,

With any form of ART, you will discover eternal OPPORTUNITIES to learn and grow,

With any form of ART, you will discover eternal THREATS to outgrow but,

In this whole voyage of discovery what you will truly discover is your authentic SELF,

To create the best version because,

The best is yet to come to live your life with fullest enthusiasm always!

So, thank you, for giving me an opportunity to guide you as Life Coach or Mentor to change the taste of your life per my best learning curves and experiences of life that I learnt, while learning to cook for my loved family and friends along with other skillsets by converting all of my wastelands into wonderland as one of the most interesting way or method to innovate or transform my authentic self into something meaningful to live meaningful life ahead.

Perhaps, you may find me speaking little extra but that's part of my authenticity and is working hard to control those extra pounds when it comes to my speaking abilities. Ha – Ha hence, kindly pardon me for consuming your little extra time and, if at any point of time you find that I have gone somewhere extra than, you may please ignore the extra side because, if it's not for you than may be for someone else needing extra care and word power to feel extra motivated to do something that he or she really wants to do in their only one *LIFE*.

So, why to waste more time, let's get started with prior cooking arrangements to get all your worries resolved in a funfilled way by helping you to learn the *"ART OF COOKING and LOVING"* the food in the most unique way so that, you can cook any delicious *DREAM LIFE* recipe in any interesting areas of your life purely your own unique way by making use of the authentic ingredients that I shared earlier for cooking any dream recipe of your life.

But, before we do that, let me give you a classic example to help you explain more, why it is important to find your true passion and highest purpose of life? Because, when you run your life with deepest passion and highest purpose of your existence, you attain personal peace as you progress authentically and when you achieve personal peace, universal peace happens at universal level. How?

The universe has five unique elements *earth, water, air, fire* and *space*. Right?

Let us assume, the passion or purpose of each element is to give freedom and to spread love, joy, peace and prosperity unconditionally being compassionate, loving, caring and big – heart generous soul so that, they can make each others existence more meaningful and beautiful in unique ways and can make their own world a better place to live in.

Likewise, the world we live in is just like the universe wherein, all human beings are like those unique elements so, if they also lead and live their life with the same passion or purpose than, imagine how beautiful their own world will be because, everyone will be able to live a more peaceful, contented and empowered life and will also be able to inspire people at large to do their best in all or any passionate interest areas of their life to spread universal peace.

Let us take the example of Mahatma Gandhi, the Father of the Indian Nation or Baapu who carried out his universal powers with his passion and purpose of life in the form of an Indian activist or an Indian freedom fighter as the leader of the Indian independence movement against British rule in India promoting non – violence, self- reliance and sustainability because he loved people compassionately and fought to set them free from british rule in India to spread love, joy, peace and prosperity in the country.

In other words, if we look at the above picture and start reading the wheel from *"Passion through Prosperity"* than these are the actual ingredients of the recipe called *"Life "*or ordinary life that he used in combination with extra ingredients of the recipe called *"Dreams,* to create an extra – ordinary authentic *"Dream Life"* recipe called *"FREEDOM"* and changed the taste of life for every citizen of the country.

KANIKA SINHA

Similarly, if we too combine the ingredients of both the recipes called *"Life"* and *"Dreams"* respectively to convert an ordinary life into an extra – ordinary life called *"Dream Life* "we can certainly change the taste of our life and others life too and can also live a content life by fulfilling our social responsibilities in the most delicious way to achieve real freedom or financial freedom for lifetime.

Hence, going with the similar thought process, I decided to add same ingredients in my dream life recipe too to live a meaningful life ahead.

As I look back today, Baapu holds a very special place in my life because August 15, India's Independence Day, marks an important event in my life too and since his teachings or words of wisdom does carry powerful message and has the power to change the people's mindset, I just thought to share everything with you here, so that, you can also try carrying out your universal powers passionately having the highest purpose of your life on this earth to have personal peace, to change the dimension of your own life in unique way by being your best self or version and to inspire people at large to be their highest self or version in their own unique way to have universal peace because,

Even if 1 percent of the population is able to attain personal peace by finding his or her truest passion and highest purpose of life, it can benefit rest of the 99 percent to have universal peace!

His most inspirational words that really inspired and touched my mind, heart, and soul are as follows:

- Your life is a message.
- Cleanliness is godliness.
- Where there is love, there is life.
- There is no god higher than truth.
- See the good in people and help them.
- In a gentle way you can shake the world.
- The future depends on what you do today.
- Without action you aren't going anywhere.
- Nobody can hurt you without your permission.
- You must be the change you want to see in the world.
- There is more to life than simply increasing its speed.
- First, they ignore you than fight with you and than you win.
- It is difficult but not impossible to conduct strictly honest business.

KANIKA SINHA

- A man is but the product of his thoughts what he thinks he becomes.
- It is better to have a heart without words than words without a heart.
- The weak can never forgive. Forgiveness is the attribute of the strong.
- The best way to find yourself is to lose yourself in the service of others.
- It is health that is your real wealth and not the pieces of gold and silver.
- Live as if you were to die tomorrow, learn as if you were to live forever.
- You should not let anyone walk through your mind with their dirty feet.
- The greatness of a nation can be judged by the way its animals are treated.
- Earth provides enough to satisfy every man's need but not every man's greed.
- If we want to reach real peace in this world, we should start educating children.
- Freedom is not worth having it, if does not include the freedom to make mistakes.

- Strength does not come from physical capacity. It comes from an indomitable will.

- Happiness is when what you think, what you say, and what you do are in harmony.

- You yourself, as much as anybody in the entire universe, deserve your love and affection.

- Whatever you believe about yourself on the inside is what you will manifest on the outside.

- If you have the belief that you can do it, you shall surely acquire the capacity to do it even if you may not have it at the beginning.

- You must not lose faith in humanity. Humanity is an ocean; if a few drops of the ocean are dirty, the ocean does not become dirty.

- Religions are different roads converging upon the same point. How does it matter if we take different roads as long as we reach the same goal.

- Strength doesn't just come from winning, your struggles develop your strength, when you go through hardships and decide not to surrender, that is strength.

And at last,

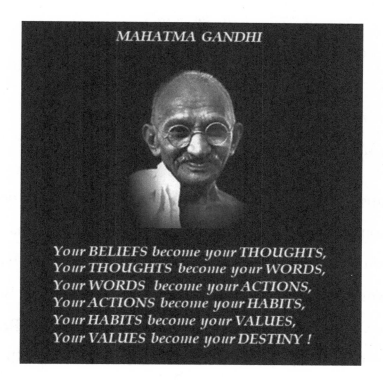

MAHATMA GANDHI

Your BELIEFS become your THOUGHTS,
Your THOUGHTS become your WORDS,
Your WORDS become your ACTIONS,
Your ACTIONS become your HABITS,
Your HABITS become your VALUES,
Your VALUES become your DESTINY !

Also, we had some other greatest leaders in the world like Dr. APJ Abdul Kalam and Martin Luther King Jr, who also carried out their social responsibilities with their passion and purpose of life and inspired millions of hearts through their actions and motivational words:

If you can't fly, than run
If you can't run, than walk
If you can't walk, than crawl

But whatever you do,

You have to keep moving forward!

also,

Darkness cannot drive out darkness; only light can do that

Hate cannot drive out hate; only love can do that!

(Martin Luther King Jr)

and to name few more we have some more inspirational personalities like my own parent Surya Prakash Sinha and Urmil Sinha (just like for any other daughter in the world because Inspiration and Education starts from Home), Brian Tracy, Zig Ziglar, Les Brown, Jyotsna Ramachandran, Robin Sharma, Dr.Willie Jolley, Sandeep Maheshwari, Shilpa Shetty, Akshay Kumar, Salman Khan, Shahrukh Khan, Amitabh Bachchan, Priyanka Chopra Jonas, Barack Obama, Narendra Modi etc. who also has been leading and living their life with passion and highest purpose of their existence or soul to make this world a better place to live in by performing the humanitarian deeds in their own respective unique ways above all challenges and limitations of their life.

So, when I read the teachings of the above-mentioned eminent personalities as a source of guidance before starting my adventurous journey, I could easily resonate my thought process with them and was able to feel more confident and uplift my positive spirit instantly. So, just the way they have their strong belief system, have passion and purpose of life or soul or existence on this earth similarly, I also have my belief system which says–

"One should live their life with fullest enthusiasm by doing everything that they are deeply passionate about but, in line with their purpose of soul or existence on this earth because, the deadly combination of passion and purpose will not only make someone fearless but, will also help in overcoming any fears and obstacles of life by breaking all sorts of mental limits purifying innerself at its best"

So, if you want to innovate or invent the best version of your authentic self to create and live an authentic dream life or extra – ordinary life your way than, my dear friend you will also have to develop an optimistic and strong belief system to design your destiny all your way that -

- Will always help you to take the control of your life.

- Will always bring and keep you closer to your highest purpose of your soul or existence on this earth.

- Will always motivate you to put your best foot forward or efforts in the right direction.

- Will always shape your thoughts based on your actions or real time experiences subsequently shaping your own unique self and

- Will always help you to create the best life for yourself and your loved ones in a beautiful way to make your own little world an authentic and a better place to live in.

Therefore, do you think that you have any strong belief system?

If yes, it's awesome but if no, don't get worried at all as we can always build one-of -a-kind at any age and stage of life provided, if we want to do so.So,let me help you by sharing my life journey that I traveled fearlessly with so much of love, fun and adventure purely my way by building my strong belief system so that, you can also try building up your own belief system to live an authentic life with your authentic self your way with much needed patience, perseverance, devotion, and determination -

- To create the best version of your *Self* through self – learning and development process beyond imagination.
- To convert any of your dreams into reality and
- To change the taste, quality and dimensions of your life forever

But, to achieve such highest level of results in return of investing your time, energy, money and hope may I ask you, to please keep your writing pad and pen ready in your hand to perform a very simple ACT that will help you to reset your life navigation system in right and clear direction and will also allow you to live a more fulfilled and meaningful life then yesterday.

Writing Pad and Pen Please!

Please know, any wish or goal or dream or purpose when written on a piece of paper all the way from your deep heart gives you the power to connect with the universe because when you start taking actions it directs your attention and focus on something you truly want and accomplish in your life having some purpose to help you feed your mind, heart and soul with optimistic energies, to move you in right direction, to connect with deepest side of your authentic self and to help you discover the highest purpose of your life as your life path you are meant to travel forever. I bet!

You can use the below LIFE PLANNER to discover your true passion and purpose of life as it helps you to stay focused all your life and helps you to realize your true potentials in all spheres of life eventually improving the quality and taste of life.

LIFE PLANNER TO CREATE YOUR NEED or DREAM LIFE											
MONTHLY - QUARTERLY - YEARLY PERFORMANCE LIFE - CYCLE											
DREAM / GOAL / WISH	WHY	ORDER OF PRIORITY	TURN AROUN D TIME	PLAN OF ACTION	JAN - FEB - MAR	STATUS	APR - MAY - JUN	STATUS	JUL - AUG - SEP	STATUS	OCT - NOV - DEC	FINAL STATUS as on last day of the year	REASON
						In - Progress		In - Progress		In - Progress		In - Progress	
						Achieved		Achieved		Achieved		Achieved	
						If carried forward, understand the gaps and repeat the performance life - cycle		If carried forward, understand the gaps and repeat the performance life - cycle		If carried forward, understand the gaps and repeat the performance life - cycle		If carried forward, understand the gaps and repeat the performance life - cycle	

So, if you really want to beautify your innerself, you will have to do it my dear friend as anything or everything that you wants to do in your life if not written anywhere can remain like an unfulfilled wish in your beautiful mind and heart and you may have to regret it later for not doing at any future stage of your life than, why not to write it down NOW to avoid any feeling of resentments later so, pick up your writing pad and pen and start writing down all your wishes or goals or dream to convert everything into reality by keeping a close track on all your minor and major accomplishments of your life to uplift your mind, heart and soul like never before because -

A DREAM written down with a date becomes a GOAL,

A GOAL broken down into steps becomes a PLAN,

A PLAN backed by ACTION becomes a REALITY!

And, when you recycle and reassemble your thoughts to convert any of your *DREAMS* into *REALITY*, Accomplish *GOALS* through *PLANS* and execute *PLANS* through your own *ACTIONS*, you may find yourself in a wonderland just like *"ALICE IN WONDERLAND"* .... *Ha- Ha!*

So, are you ready to create or write or share your own life story of personal transformation after accomplishing all your minor or major goals or purpose or dreams?

If yes, it's awesome but if no, than you should start writing all your minor or major wishes from now on instead of just nodding your head and making unhappy faces without wasting your precious time because –

TIME IS PRECIOUS AND IS EVERYTHING!

And, if you too agree with it, this is the time to start converting all your dreams into reality.

Let's do it NOW!

Half of what I have said in this book, may seem meaningless unless you "DO" but, I have said it, so that the other half may reach out to you when you really "DO", and that is only possible when you agree to travel the distance between "DO" and "DO" to discover your true passion and highest purpose of life to continue your doings in the right direction.

The voice of life in me can only reach the ear of life in you if, we promise each other to connect through our heart and soul so,

It doesn't matter which place we all are coming from because, what really matters is the spiritual connect that should happen between our mind, heart and soul.

Having said that and going forward with the same mindset, every person in this world belongs to some beautiful place so do I, hence, it gives me an immense pleasure to share with you that, I belong to a city called Moradabad, Uttar Pradesh, Northern India, which is popularly known as "The Brass City" for its famous brass handicrafts distributed worldwide ranging home décor products.

I did my schooling from St Mary's Convent Senior Secondary School, Moradabad than, did my graduation from Graphic Era Deemed University, Dehradun and than did my Post Graduation from Singhad Institute of Management, Pune.

After completing my postgraduate studies and earning my master's in personnel (Human Resources) management, I got my first professional career break as a management trainee in the telecommunications industry based out in Delhi, where I worked very hard like any other fresher would do and as a result of investing my time, energy, money and hope in something that I liked doing, the very best thing that happened with me was, I got absorbed by the company as an executive in human resources and than got promoted as a Senior human resources executive officer with so many additional monetary and non - monetary rewards and recognitions as a good start of career life.

Being an ambitious soul, I was looking for advancement in roles and responsibilities but circumstances didn't allow me to continue with my tenure within the same organization as my destiny had something better in store for me.

February 21,2009, marked the beginning of my new life. How?

Since my father knew about my foodie spirit so, before letting me know about the actual reason (marriage) of travel, he asked, do you want to go to Hyderabad for eating world famous scrumptious Biryani? I said yes, out of sheer excitement. Ha – Ha!

Because, what else an ardent foodie like me would say who can travel miles with smile on her face to enjoy something that she loves or is passionate about even though it means long distance travelling i.e. from Northern India, New Delhi to Southern India, Hyderabad.

After taking break and exploring Hyderabad for six months post marriage, I wanted to resume with work to continue with my professional endeavors being a workaholic in nature so, I started looking for a job and fortunately was able to get a job in an ITES (Information Technology Enabled Services) company as a Process Lead and since was a performer so being a returning employee I did well and was promoted to next level as an Associate Process Manager for my exceptional performance as a full - time employee.

A few months later, came the worst phase of my life which taught me to take good care of myself as I never cared too much about my health being intensely involved in my studies and work. Perhaps, that was not the right time to get started with my real career life. My health had deteriorated so much that I could not concentrate on my work for quite long time and when I rejoined things had changed so, I had to accept the kind of responsibilities that I didn't like at all and was desperately looking for a change because there was no room for further advancement, but again, I could not do it since Universe had some better plans for me as I moved to USA for beginning of the new best life.

As I remember, before moving to the USA, one of my colleague questioned me, what would I do post moving there? I said, will pursue my other interests because for me life is not only limited to the corporate world rather life is also about exploring the other side of the world too, to experience overall growth and to live a content life forever. So, having this mindset, we moved to United States for better employment opportunity lined up for my spouse with one of the biggest online retail giant in the world to move life at next level and to accomplish another dream or wish or goal as per my "LIFE PLANNER".

So, after moving to the USA, we started exploring the new life, new culture, multicultural cuisines, met variety of people hailing from diverse cultures, surroundings and many beautiful places in and outside the city we lived in like many other people do when they travel abroad so that, we can understand and immerse in the new culture comfortably and than, after sometime I left for India and Australia to spend good quality time with my family as I missed them so much post moving to the United States for the first time in my life.

Feeling little relaxed and after coming back to USA after long break of 8 months, I explored more states and cities and than decided to add more feathers to my achievers cap in a different way to live a more content life and to innovate my strongest self then yesterday so, that was the time when I actually wanted to get on to the path of spirituality or do self – enlightenment.

Now, let me give you some brief awareness about what spirituality or self – enlightenment is?

Spirituality is a natural function, a state of reconnection with the self, with our essence. In order to find and develop it, we must take a fresh look on who we are, our lives, and focus on the essence.

Going through a spiritual awakening is one of the most confusing, lonely, alienating, but also supremely beautiful experiences in life because - Spirituality is the gift of love. Service to others is the discipline of love. If you reach out often to those in need, not because you should but because your heart leads you more and more deeply into the hearts of others than keep on going as spirituality is a path of high self-esteem. The spiritual approach to Universe, is one remaining in that self-esteem and cultivating a relationship that is as real, direct and as dynamic as we might have with a member of our family, a friend or a companion.

So, gradually, I started exploring my creative abilities passionately to stay more mentally active until I discover the deepest passion and highest purpose of my life on this earth or connects spiritually with my deepest self to live my life with fullest enthusiasm always, as I truly believe we all have been sent here to fulfill some purpose—it's just that we need to dig deep inside us to find and live a meaningful life forever.

My continuous intense positive actions as self-fulfillment pleasures –

- Helped me to overcome mental depression arising out of grey weather conditions of the city we lived in.
- Helped me to develop an optimistic and strong belief system subsequently.
- Helped me to discover multiple talents inside me as a resourceful human being.
- Helped me to establish my value system or pillars of strength and also
- Helped me to expand my horizons and skills in different interest areas of life like Food, Fitness, Fashion, Home Decor, Photography and Writing.

After having so much of fun in different areas, I thought why not to further hone few of my gifted talents and take life to the next level of happiness and contentment through stages of progression optimistically and patiently so that, I could again get on to the path of true financial independence and freedom by doing something different this time means pursuing my most passionate interest areas that could also offer best of my services to the outside world as my social responsibility as a compassionate human being in different way so, as a result, I started thinking deeply about all of my interests areas so that, my deepest interest can help me to become the best version of my authentic self and can help others as well to re–define the dimensions of their life through my best possible creative efforts in right direction because-

> *Direction is much more important than speed,*
> *Many are going nowhere fast despite of putting*
> *extraordinary efforts obsessively! (Zig Ziglar)*

Now, since all of my chosen interest areas required certain amount of investment in the form of time, energy, money and hope so, before advancing my passionate areas to next level and thinking from long term perspective considering my personal needs I did further deep analysis to set the utmost clarity of WHY because if your why is clear, your HOW becomes easy and you can always increase the dimensions of your life accordingly by setting up minor and major goals at your end to channelize your creative energies in much optimum ways and to emerge as one of the strongest ambiversion of your true self.

So, below were my simple and clear WHY's or purpose or minor goals to get me started from somewhere for my very own personal transformation while enjoying the life with everything I just liked doing as my hobby having deep faith in my optimistic belief – system -

FOOD and FITNESS – To create healthy food recipes for my family and friends because "Health is real Wealth".

HOME DECOR – To decorate my living ambience by adding personal touch to my home surroundings and to contribute my best in achieving financial goals at family level.

TRAVELLING – To travel around and to experience the real treasures of the world with my family and friends.

PHOTOGRAPHY – To capture the natural beauty of the world and create memories to freeze the golden moments of life for life so that when I look back can always cherish beautiful memories for lifetime.

MOTIVATIONAL WRITING – To help people as much as I can in some form like sharing material or content helping to improve the quality of life through social media platforms like Facebook and Instagram.

100% confusion gets clear when we think deeply about our actions what we have already done, is doing or wanting to do having some purpose in life so, it is critically important to know your WHY's so that, we can live our life with deepest love, joy, peace and prosperity forever because, once we feel clear headed and start achieving our why's one by one through greatest amount of patience and perseverance we can always break our mental limits or boundaries and can increase the dimensions of our life to raise level of happiness and contentment everyday but, we will have to keep moving by all means consistently if we truly wants to fill our real life with much more happiness and contentment that we deserve at our best so,

If you are passionate about everything you love doing, just keep removing the layers of THOUGHTS through CYCLE – OF– ACTIONS continuously

to find your true PASSION and highest PURPOSE

of your life because -

Passion, Purpose, Positivity, Patience, Perseverance,
Progression, Perfection, Performance,
Power, People and Profits define the universal
growth and dimensions of life !

Life

© LIFE PHOTOGRAPHY

You don't need a strong "WHY" behind, you need a strong "WHY" forward!

(Damien Rider)

So, How about your – *self?*

If you know your WHY's too, it's awesome but if No, than NOW is the time to find out as there are many people in this world who does lot of work but sometimes fail because they lack clarity of their WHY's so, you just have to do a deep analysis about all of your actions so far to find out the reason behind it just the way I did to define my basic purpose to get me started from somewhere and to subsequently discover my highest purpose of life by listening to my deepest inner voice.

So, If you are a serious – minded, highly ambitious, growth - oriented individual and is ready to build your spiritual belief and value system or thoughts and is also ready to find your true passion and highest purpose of your life through one of the most cost-effective method of self - education without spending dollar or cent than, let me share my wins and takeaways after practicing this method of self - education at my best above all other challenges of life as an opportunists to help you understand in detail that when you practice power of alphabetical series how universe helps you to transform yourself into something meaningful to let you live your life with fullest enthusiasm always.

KANIKA SINHA

CHAPTER – IV

PART - 1

Self – Learning - Travel Far Enough you meet your "Self" to discover your soul purpose

My WINS & TAKEAWAYS

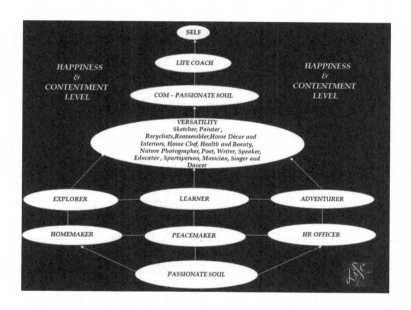

Though your PURPOSE imposes certain limits and defines dimensions of your life at first place

*but, your PASSION always gives you power to
break and re – define your limits and dimensions
of your life so, make sure your passion for your
purpose should always be greater in your life to
find and live a meaningful life ahead with highest
purpose to make you unstoppable.*

Going with the same mindset, this picture reflects highest level of my authentic self or my best version so far after using the same delicious authentic ingredients of recipes called *life* and *dream* respectively to create my *dreamlife* recipe that you are reading now. Hence, If you too want to have your best version in some way or create any other dream life recipe in your life, than you may also start pursuing any of your interest area or areas passionately after defining your purpose or knowing your WHY's deeply using the same ingredients because, you never know when, any of your likes helps you to discover your true passion and highest purpose of your life or bring you closer to next level of your highest self because to every level there is next hidden higher and highest level so, when you reach your highest level than you are in the process of making the best version of yourself or true self to take life altogether at next level.

Let's say,

If your passion and purpose is to become a Sketcher than, your next level could be to become a Painter.

If your passion and purpose is to become a Recyclist or Re – Assembling expert than, your next level could be to become a Home Décor Artist.

If your passion and purpose is to become a Home Décor Artist than, your next level could be to become a Home Décor and Interior Artist.

If your passion and purpose is to cook delicious food for your family and friends as Home Chef than, your next level could be to become a World Class Chef or Open your own Restaurant or to start your own cooking shows or YouTube Channel.

If your passion and purpose is to become Hair and Makeup expert than, your next level could be to open your own Saloon or Hair & Beauty Institute.

If your passion and purpose is to become a Nature Photographer than, your next level could be to open your own Photography studio.

If your passion and purpose is to become a Poet or Writer than, your next level could be to become an Author or anything else.

If your passion and purpose is to become a Musician than, your next level could be to become a professional versatile musician.

If your passion and purpose is to become a Singer and Dancer than, your next level could be to become a professional singer or choreographer or to open your own institute

If you have any other passion and purpose of life other than the one mentioned above than continue doing until you discover your next level as the list could be endless.

So, just keep on trying and don't worry about the perfections rather worry about staying progressive by all means as much as you can to discover the highest purpose of your authentic self-ONE day and to subsequently become the best version of your best self through perseverance everyday then yesterday.

Just keep progressing with patience every single day in whatever areas you like or love doing to reach at your higher or highest self and to take your life at next level giving you infinite opportunities to utilize all your creative energies in its most optimum ways with much clearer and more focused mind to convert all your dreams into reality because when -

Progress meets Progress, Progress meets Perfection!
(Kanika Sinha)

And, how you can progress or stay in progressive mode to achieve your passion and purpose of life, let's continue the reading fun.

We have three categories of people –

Category A – Focus on Family needs

Category B – Focus on Family and Friends needs and

Category C – Focus on Family, Friends and Universe needs

When I did my self - analysis, I found myself belonging to Category A initially and than slowly and steadily moved my focus to Category B and than to Category C to create my best version.

Nothing happened overnight as it took me four good years to transform myself into something meaningful but, that doesn't mean that you will also take same amount of time to shape your best self as not everybody has similar challenging situations and circumstances in life.

So, How about your – self?

Which category you belong to? Because, if you know the limits of your focus area you can always break all your limits through your intense actions and can drive your life with much higher or highest purpose of life with much clear and focused mind passionately therefore,

WHERE and HOW much you invest your time, energy, money and hope will genuinely determine your results to make progress every day with focused mind.

If we invest our time, energy, money and hope in something we love doing passionately every day, positive results are guaranteed provided, we should maintain our patience level as high as possible until we get to see the results either expected or beyond expectations or imaginations to experience the heavenly journey of life because your actions will always guide you to become better, better and better version of yours until you discover your highest self and will help you to advance the best version of your true or highest self if your soul promise to progress.

Hence, to maintain the continuity of intense actions, we should know some critical facts about human body as in how it can work effectively and progressively in any toughest situation of life to be the winner in any or every stage of life.

So, do you know which is the most powerful part of the human body?

Well, to me it's the BRAIN, because that has made me the much stronger person and version that I am today.

You have to train your mind to be stronger than your emotions else you'll lose yourself every time!

Yes, that's true so, let us study how we can do so to become the kind of personality you wish to see yourself in this only life because you can achieve anything if you put your mind, heart and soul together in everything that you love. I bet!

Our mind is a powerful source of information so, when you fill it with positive thoughts or positive knowledge your life will start to change because -

The only way that we can live is, if we grow,
The only way that we can grow is, if we change,
The only way that we can change is, if we learn,
The only way we can learn is, if we are exposed,

And, the only way that we can become exposed is,

If we throw ourselves out into the ocean,

Do it! if you can, to reach where you want to be!

So, the very first step to change your mind, in some way is, you must be open to new thoughts, new interpretations, new perceptions, as your life around you will only change when you will allow change for what's going on inside of you because that will keep you mentally, emotionally, morally, spiritually, physically, intellectually and financially strong hence it should be our prime duty to take care of our mental health in the best possible way to live a healthy and wealthy life forever.

Now, to enlighten your mind with something that can keep you fit and hit all the time in all of your interesting areas of life is my caring area so, just thought, why not to pen down some of the most important learnings from my personal experiences that can help and benefit you in the best possible ways and you too can enlighten and empower your mind just the way I did, or maybe in some better ways because everything starts from the self, so let's fly, means first love your – *self* -

Self
Be Your – Self
Love Your – Self
Trust Your – Self
Bless Your – Self
Value Your – Self
Accept Your – Self
Express Your – Self
Educate Your - Self
Evaluate Your – Self
Enlighten Your – Self
Entertain Your - Self
Empower Your – Self
To be the best version of your True – Self !

And, make the difference in your own life and in others life because -

Yesterday is gone and tomorrow may never come so, why not put some extra efforts with the help of authentic mentors that can bring more life to your existence to beautify your inner and outer self in such a way that it increases your self-worth and credibility more with each passing day.

Now, that you know about my crazy taste buds so, if you are a foodie just like me, than let me help you to understand from an ardent foodie perspective more as for some people food is life and for some it's not but, for sure an important part of everyday life that works like oxygen and without which no one can survive for long.

So, what if, we get to eat our favorite home cooked authentic food in versatile flavors every day than we will not just survive but will thrive in rocking way every single day if we are ready to put some extra efforts above all sorts of daily challenges in life to live healthy lifestyle always.

And, if we are ready to do so, than let me take you to my world of authentic flavors to share the most delicious ingredients that I used to change the taste of my life and to learn some amazing cooking or life tips that I learned during my self - learning and development process to help you discover your life path through your progressive efforts at your end with each passing day just the way I discovered because –

Staying progressive is much more important than being a perfectionist, as progressiveness always gives you scope to become perfectionist with time once you choose your life path with clear mind! (Kanika Sinha)

So, keep walking until the fog gets over to see clear life path ahead!

Although, this world is the land of versatile flavors, wherever we travel in this world but, if sometimes we really want to enjoy authentic and traditional flavors from different cuisines of the world than, the easiest and the most cost-effective way to do so is to cook by yourself with all of your favorite special herbs and spices and this is only possible if you have enough time and knowledge of all the delicious ingredients that goes into your authentic dream recipe of life.

What if, you have the time but you do not have the knowledge of those special ingredients? Than, you would probably look out for some restaurants serving authentic and traditional food or will ask your close friends and family members to cook for you or will refer some recipe book that will help you to satisfy those intense cravings. Right?

Likewise, if you crave to make your version as the best version just like any other authentic recipe than you can easily do so, if you have extra time and knowledge of all the essential ingredients but, what if you have the time but you lack knowledge that can make your life worth living? Than, you would probably look out for some life improvement course or hire a professional coach or read books on personal and professional development by some of the famous authors in the world. Right?

Now, given the health challenges in everyday life each one of us want to live a healthy lifestyle to keep our energy levels as high as possible so, the best way to overcome any health challenge is to kill those intense cravings by either referring to some recipe book to cook healthy food at home and to use your own creativity skills or simply sit back and feel sad for not getting something to eat that you are genuinely craving for so, let's say if you choose to utilize your time in a better way means cooking for yourself, you are all set to create the world best authentic healthy recipe for life just like my version of *Moradabadi Biryani*....Ha - Ha !

Hence, going with my preferred choices, I chose to cook healthy meals for myself and for my family instead eating outside food daily from a restaurant, to enjoy the best authentic and traditional healthy food and to have the most wonderful time together always to satisfy those intense cravings above all sorts of challenges in everyday life in a country home away from home.

Likewise, if you want to make your version the best version in any areas of life, you will have to utilize your time by doing something extra at your end and when you do so and get successful, you should also try to share the ingredients further with your loved ones with the belief that sharing is caring and life becomes more meaningful and satisfying because the family and friends that eat together, support, encourage and motivates each other for what they do, will always stay together and will always share a special bond of relationship lifelong because the act of sharing is the sign of generous heart wanting to make others grow as well along with their self-growth and development as a compassionate human being to help people experience the life from a different perspective.

So, are you compassionate enough to infuse your passion in the life of your loved ones? If yes, it's awesome but if No, than just don't worry you can always do it if you desire, decide and is determined to so.

Now, since daily investment of time and energy made me better happier version of myself as a Home - Chef for my family and friends then yesterday so, to fuel my passion more I decided to refer some recipe books as my mentor or guide to become the best version of myself in some unique ways.

So, while honing my cooking skills what I learned was, as cooking or life tip –

FOOD and LIFE taste more delicious when we add SALT or CHALLENGE to satisfy those mouth watering cravings despite of having all ingredients !

©LIFE PHOTOGRAPHY

Agree? Yes, I know because, even though our food will have all the necessary delicious ingredients, it will always taste less delicious in the absence of salt similarly, until we add challenges to our life, our life will never taste more delicious that's why, I always believe challenges are the way to make the best ambiversion of ourself because -

Challenges will break and shake your mind, heart and soul infinite times but will definitely shape you to become the best version of your true self !
(Kanika Sinha)

Now, that we understand the importance of salt in food so cooking regular meals or three-course or a five-course meal or writing motivational quotes or articles in everyday life cannot be the challenge anymore for any one of us but cooking a thirty-course or a fifty-course meal or writing a book could be when it comes to serving our friends, family and world at a large scale. Right? Hence, I decided to attempt a challenge of cooking thirty-course or a fifty-course meal or to write a book to hone my cooking or writing skills to next level and to enjoy my life more with each passing day to become the better version of my authentic self then yesterday as a World Class Chef or Life Coach to feed your mind, heart and soul with positive knowledge every day.

As I love reading too so, while reading some general books, I came across one of the powerful cooking or life tip by Thought Architect Coach, Deepak N Raghava which infused my mind just like an incredible aroma:

"Your materialistic looks may enhance your own appearance but, your thoughts can enlighten others"!

Which means, if we only focus on our self-development, we may have typical selfish or self–centered outlook towards life but, if we change our perspective to win – win situation, we can live one of the most fulfilling life as a compassionate human being on this earth as it will allow us to live a more meaningful life and will also give us an opportunity to practice an authentic leadership style in an authentic and compassionate way. I bet!

So, to bring that change within ourself, let us take a look at Maslow's Hierarchy of needs to know and understand, up to what extent we should travel as much as we can to utilize our energies in its most optimum ways to become the best version of ourself -

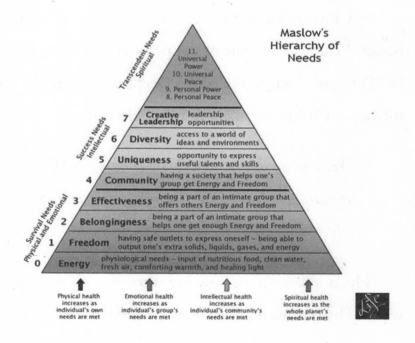

Looking at the diagram, up to what extent or level you would like to utilize your energies or positive energies is absolutely your choice but you can always try to aim high, as high as possible and try changing the outlook to feel the difference in your own life to experience deepest level of personal peace and universal peace at universal level to live life universe size having universal powers at its best.

Just like the perfect ingredients to change the taste of my life some powerful words again made me feel confident about my thinking process that –

Words do have the power to change the taste or quality of life because what and how you think clearly matters the most above all xyz reasons. So, if we keep our mind filled with intensely delicious ingredients called powerful words with there powerful meanings our life will become intensely delicious and powerful too to enjoy extremely good taste of life hence some powerful words or ingredients and my continuous actions helped me to discover, advance and develop myself to next level having the minimalist approach in life every time I tried something new.

Just the way, we make use of delicious ingredients to cook any authentic and traditional recipe for our family and friends similarly, to create better or best version of ourself, to change the taste, quality and dimensions of life and to make this world a better place to live in, we should make efforts to serve the society at large as well and to do so, we should thoroughly prepare our mind as early as possible with some positive facts so that we should not feel stuck anywhere in the journey of life to leave a powerful impact wherever our life or destiny takes us around the world because -

We cannot predict the future, but we certainly have an authentic power to create one-of-a -kind through love, hard work and perseverance! (Kanika Sinha)

And, how we can do so let's keep reading further.

PART - 2

We all have two lives,

The second one starts when we realize we only have one!

Yes, that's true, the first part of our life we have already lived probably with XYZ reasons, but the second part of our life we can still live with some meaningful reason given the opportunity or by creating an opportunity all by ourselves because –

> *Where there is LOVE, there is WILL,*
> *Where there is WILL, there is WAY,*
> *Where there is WAY, there is COURAGE ,*
> *Where there is COURAGE, there is POWER ,*
> *Where there is POWER, there is DETERMINATION ,*
> *Where there is DETERMINATION, Every impossible thing is POSSIBLE,*
> *When you achieve something IMPOSSIBLE, you become UNSTOPPABLE !*

And, when you become unstoppable that state could be the state of self-realization, or state of awakening, or state of progression, which can occur in any stage of your life, be it first or second but it should happen at some point of life to accomplish the highest level of peace inside you.

No one changes unless they want to. There is only one thing that makes someone change. Their own realization that they need to do it. And there's only one time it will happen when they decide they are ready (Lory Deschene)

I got that moment of realization in my life when I was 32 years old and was looking for the deepest self-enlightenment to recreate a successful career path for myself with something I am deeply in love with.

But, in order to do so, what was much needed was the courage to invest quality time on myself to do something creatively different by exploring all of my interest passionately and than choosing something that my soul would want to pursue rest of my life with the fullest enthusiasm having highest purpose of life after having served the corporate world for a good five years as a management trainee, human resources executive, a senior human resources executive, a process lead, an associate process manager with much more accolades as a fulltime employee.

So, getting five promotions in total employment span of five years was another set of dreams or wish or goals that came true after investing my time, energy, money and hope.

Now, you must be thinking why I explored and is asking you to do the same courageous task at your end too, if possible?

Well, the answer is simply beautiful, as for sure it will make you an elegant piece of indomitable strength, if you truly want to do something better then what you did yesterday to become your best version beyond imagination because -

Your *life* is important,

Your *dreams* are important,

Your *story* is important,

Your *voice* is important,

You were born to make an *impact* in this only life!

> *"One day you will wake up and there won't be any more time to do the things you've always wanted to do. Do it now"* (Paulo Coelho)

So, please continue to read the contents of this book with an open mind and heart and listen to the deepest inner voice of your soul, as it could be your true calling!

- What is that one thing, or maybe several other things, that you always wanted to do but could not do it for XYZ reasons?

- Maybe you want to do something that you have been thinking about for a while but need courage or mentoring?

- Maybe you are not at all serious about your life, but may get after reading this book?

Take some time out from your regular routine and think about –

- What you are or have been doing?

- Why you are doing and is that really keeping your soul happy and content?

Write down everything at a writing pad, as it activates the neuromotor of physical activity and let your mind think in a very different and positive way and when you do so, than please congratulate yourself for taking one of the best steps of your life to create the best version ahead exactly the way you want to, so visualize it NOW.

After finding answers to all of the above questions, if all of your answers are positive than keep doing what you have been doing but, if all or any of the answer is negative, than it's time to act now, or never, as I did four years ago, since I always believed that self or personal development is much more important than any professional development and this is only possible if we have the courage to invest some time on ourselves by exploring, experiencing, enlightening, educating and empowering our mind with real-time knowledge so that we can embrace more passionate and fulfilled life than ever because-

> *Jobs only fill your pocket but adventures fill your soul and*
> *When your soul is filled with contentment, the journey of life becomes extraordinary! (Kanika Sinha)*

So, do you love yourself to the extent of taking a calculative risk to find out what you love doing the most in order to innovate or invent your new best version despite of your current situation or any limitations and challenges in your life to create and live your dream life your way?

If the answer is yes, let's keep going, as I am sure you will also start chasing your dreams with much more confidence to make the difference in your own life and in others lives in best way.

> *Don't let your limitations define your aspirations rather let your aspirations break all your limitations! (Kanika Sinha)*

As, Mr. Brian Tracy, an American – Canadian motivational speaker and self – development author rightly says –

> *Do something every day to move yourself towards your major goal by accepting and overcoming challenges or limitations to surpass your goal!*

For Example - If we think about swimming activity what does it teaches us?

If we can swim in a pool as a minor goal, we can swim in the ocean too as a major goal hence,

If swimming in a pool needs an ordinary courage than, by having some extraordinary courage we can swim any size of the ocean. Right?

So, having said that, lets assume, "minor goals" are the way of accomplishing needs of life and "major goals " are the way of accomplishing the dreams of life hence, to fulfill minor goals or needs, you may just need an ordinary courage and strength but to fulfill your major goals or dreams you would definitely need an extraordinary courage and strength but, this is only possible if you are ready to invest extra time, energy and positive hope to build that extra worth of yourself either through some mentorship program or any self-development exercise.

If you have loads of money, developing yourself through a mentorship program will probably be the easiest option but, what if you have money but your other priorities does not allow you to make any other necessary investments or you have tight budget? Than, the best way is to invest time, energy and hope on yourself is through self – help to become much stronger or better or new version then you were yesterday and

If you are to do that, than how you can do it?

Let me guide you with that process, my dear friend.

Life is like the ocean,
It can be calm or still,
Rough or rigid,
But in the end, it is always beautiful!

Also,

You will never cross the ocean unless you have the
courage to lose sight of the shore!

For a swimmer, assessing the depth of the pool can be an easygoing activity to achieve minor goal of swimming in the pool but assessing the size and depth of the ocean at first place may look like an easygoing activity because of the depth finder device but, achieving the major goal of crossing the ocean or diving up to the ground surface of the ocean could certainly be one of the biggest challenge. Right?

To beat the challenge, measuring the depth of the ocean is an important driving factor for the ones who love swimming so that, they can proactively prepare themselves with an extraordinary strength and energy that they would need to swim an ocean.

So, if you are a swimmer, your highest aim or purpose or major goal should either be to reach the ground surface of the ocean floor to enjoy the deepest dive or to cross any ocean irrespective of size needing extra – ordinary strength and courage. Likewise, if you are a true adventurer, an explorer, an undying learner and is obsessed about creating the best life for yourself and your loved ones by becoming the best version of your true self than, your major goal should be to reach the roots or ground surface of your soul means to connect with your deepest self because that will give you magical powers to distinguish yourself from others in a positive and healthy way and will help you to find and live the highest purpose of your soul or true existence on this earth in an extra -ordinary and courageous way.

Therefore, going with the above mind-set and being a fearless swimmer, measuring the depth of an artistic ocean inside me was important to find out so that, I can become the best ambiversion and authentic version of my true self and can balance my life in best possible way being highly active and restless in nature because, if you know and understand the difference between what you like and what you love, every pressure will feel like a pleasure, and you can swim any ocean irrespective of any size with an extraordinary courage. I bet!

For Example, when we like a flower, we just pluck it. But when we love a flower, we water it daily despite of knowing the fact that every single or other day we will have to spend time in watering our garden for long hours.

There is a beautiful saying that goes –

You are the creator of your own life garden,
Plant kindness and compassion,
Water with love and gratitude,
And, you will enjoy the beauty all the days of your
life!

So, when you love doing something passionately every single or other day you will always come out as a winner no matter how much time goes into it to create the best life garden for yourself filled with your favorite flowers, plants, trees, fruits, vegetables or something else that you would love to see every second, every minute, and every day either as life or part of your life. I bet!

You know what?

KANIKA SINHA

The greatest pleasure in swimming an ocean lies, when you are not a trained swimmer and you need to learn swimming all by your self with fearless attitude to reach your destination !

©LIFE PHOTOGRAPHY

Sounding a bit scary? Yeah, I know, my dear friend, but that's how my thrilling and adventurous experience has been on my incredible authentic journey of enlightenment and empowerment to discover my new authentic *self* and all I can say is that, it was one of the most amazing journeys of my life because, the way my soul feels so deeply content today was not four years back.

Yes, that's true!

At first place, making a big life change looked scary to me as well but again, after considering an excellent cooking or life tip from Robin Sharma, The Canadian Writer –

"Any change is hard at first, messy in the middle, and gorgeous at the end "

I kept moving, as I didn't want to waste my life by apologizing, regretting, questioning, or hating myself later in any stage of my life because I knew what could be scarier. Regret! of not doing something that I could have been deeply passionate about if, I would have explored my deepest self!

So, while accomplishing all of my WHY's or minor goals or need through cooking, sketching, painting, re–assembling, recycling or converting wasteland into wonderland, travelling, photography and writing to keep my creative mind active as high as high possible during my learning and development process and in the hope of living a content life, I eventually discovered my true passion and highest purpose of life as my social responsibility or met my true SELF or soul purpose of life i.e –

To educate, enlighten, empower, encourage and entertain human mind, heart and soul for deepest personal peace boosting self - growth and development at personal and universe level believing -

Life is too short to wake up in the morning with
regret my dear friend,
If you get a chance, take it,
If it changes your life, let it,
Nobody said it would be easy,
They just promised it would be worth it!

In my life, I have met so many people who regret, literally regret, not living the life of their choice and felt empty handed despite of having everything best in their life.

So, if you too want to avoid the "feeling of emptiness" at any stages of your life, you will have to give extra hours or invest time to enlighten yourself in a better way, to put your efforts in the right direction and to shape your life in the best way but you will have to do it because there is NO EXCUSE life policy that you will have to agree with as per your own terms and conditions giving you cutting edge to drive your life all your way.

Doesn't it sounds interesting and amazing wherein you will hold an absolute right as a policy maker of your own life having your own set of terms and condition to run your day and not letting the day run you? Yes, I know, it does!

Now, how you can run your day by putting extra hours or efforts to stay in progressive mode as per your own terms and conditions could be a million-dollar question and to answer that you may need a million-dollar book or a million-dollar guide or mentor or coach to help you given the way the life challenges are demanding people to increase their self – worth and credibility with time else one may have to experience some of the worst days of life but one can still overcome any of the setbacks arising out of such situations if any by remembering that –

Sometimes you have to experience the worst days of your life to experience the best days of life!

Since I too experienced some of the worst days of my life hence, let me share my exciting,fun-filled, learning and personal transformational journey being the fearless swimmer, to give you a feel of how small or big accomplishments helped me in raising my self-worth and credibility by purely doing something I loved doing passionately every day with all my mind, heart, and soul to fulfill all my needs believing –

Patience and Perseverance are the keys to success!
(Kanika Sinha)

As, HOME CHEF– Lived my WHY, by creating more than 100 of healthy recipes to switch from unhealthy eating habits to healthy habits to adopt a healthy lifestyle because ingredients are what you buy, but cooking food with those ingredients is what you really do with it as it directly impacts your mind, heart, body, and soul so, do watch your food intake sharply to stay healthy and wealthy all your life.

Sharing snapshots of few of my creations for your easy reference –

Also,

Your diet is not only what you eat.

It's what you watch, what you listen to, what you
read, the people you hang around!
(Zig Ziglar)

So, be mindful of the things you put into your body emotionally, spiritually and physically.

As, HOME DECOR ARTISTS – Lived my WHY by creating more than 100 of home décor products for my living space by converting all of my wasteland into wonderland through recycling and reassembling and was subsequently able to sell my hand – made products to people at large.

Sharing snapshot of few of my creations while exploring my creative abilities at home decor front –

As, TRAVELLER and PHOTOGRAPHER – Lived my WHY by travelling to more than 100 favorite places around the world and captured 1000 pictures of the real treasures of the world in an artistic way to cherish golden memories for lifetime.

Sharing snapshot of some of my favorite places that I visited along with my family and friends –

As, MOTIVATIONAL WRITER – Lived my WHY by sharing 1000 of motivational quotes during my self - learning and development process and by writing blogs and free articles through my page on social media platforms like Facebook and Instagram. So, please express your love by liking my page and to connect with me directly through my public account "LIFE – Live it with fullest Enthusiasm34" on Facebook and life_live_it_to_the-fullest34 as Kanika Sinha (Nika) on Instagram if you enjoyed reading my book.

Have mentioned few of my favorite quotes which you have already read by now and hope should help you too to learn and grow with time the way it helped me to grow.

And, the next big ocean that I eventually swimmed and that made me the better version of myself as a whole then yesterday is,

As, an AUTHOR – Lived my WHY by recycling and reassembling my thought process through all of my creations and released my first book to experience the next high level of happiness and contentment as a motivational writer through patience and perseverance creating the best life path for myself from being free to financially free once again and to subsequently help me to accomplish another bigger dream of mine.

So, as a result of my continuous efforts another cooking or life tip that I learned was –

Until you do something that you love doing of whatsoever nature, you will never know your limits because the secret of success is found in the little pleasures of life as it always gives you universal power to re - define your limits by giving you infinite opportunities to become the best version of yourself !

©LIFE PHOTOGRAPHY

If the contents of this book can push and break my mental limits to experience the real meaning of versatility than it can help anybody but this will only happen when you will also try to execute the knowledge that you will learn through this book if you too want to feed your soul more than your ego of earning only money using inappropriate ways because-

"A satisfied life is always better than a successful life, as our success is measured by others, but our own satisfaction is measured by our mind, heart, and soul "!

Remember, we are the ones who knows better whats going inside of us better than anybody else in the world.

When you set and accomplish any of your minor or major goals through hard work and perseverance, you may experience multiple levels of happiness and contentment because to every level you may find the scope of improvement and advancement so, if you continue to put your endless efforts with patience until you reach your highest self believe me the taste, quality and dimensions of your life will never be the same again, as it will make you feel not less than an achiever or winner in all areas of your life.

Another cooking or life tip that I learned from a very senior person in my field of expertise to raise the altitude of my version is -

*The **mediocre** teacher tells,*
*The **good** teacher explains,*
*The **superior** teacher demonstrates and,*
*The **great** teacher inspires through their actions!*

So, which version would you like to be? The choice is yours, but whatever you choose, please ensure that it should deeply enlighten everyone whomsoever you meet in your life as it doesn't matter what version you would you like to be but, it does matter how much you have enlightened and empowered yourself to empower others compassionately so, keep experimenting in the areas of life that you love doing the most until you break your mental limits or past records to inspire others and to live a healthy lifestyle absolutely your own unique way to be your best version.

Now, I have some more questions for you so that, you are pretty much confident by now and is ready to get into the mood of reading some more serious content.

If you can answer it well, you are all set to change your world too:

- Are you seriously wanting to change the taste, quality and dimensions of your life by becoming the best version of yourself through any of your interest areas?

- Do you want to be an inspiring teacher in any chosen interest of yours to work like a guiding force for people looking for helping hands?

- Do you want to become financially free and live more useful or respectful life because financial independence is paramount to live your life on your own terms and conditions?

If the answer is yes, to all the above questions, that means my friend already knows what he or she expects out of this single blessed life. It's awesome !

But, if No for any reason than, don't worry and get up now and tell yourself "You can do it" because you have what it takes to be at your true or highest self-it's just that you have to keep trying by pushing your mental limits.

Please know my dear friend, that abundance of love, joy, peace, and prosperity will only come into existence if you are ready to understand and promise yourself that this is my life and I am going to be the driver of my own life with the highest sense of ownership and responsibility and will do whatever efforts it will demand to accomplish all of my minor or major goals in any areas of my life.

So, another cooking or life tip that I have for you is -

Continuous Learning and Development, Growth and
Expansion results in Abundance of Joy and Optimism !

© LIFE PHOTOGRAPHY

In my life journey, I also went through some of the craziest roller-coaster experiences because I was trying to live more content life by swimming all sizes of pools and oceans with fearless attitude since I always believed that -

Life is just like a roller-coaster experience,
Either you scream or you enjoy the ride!

It's absolutely your choice!

So, I kept moving further by enjoying my roller-coaster ride optimistically because that's when I took the help from reliable mentor and friend called *"BRAIN"* as a lifesaving jacket which helped me to swim all of my small or big size pool or ocean in an easygoing way believing -

The choice is yours, because it's your life and your choice!

So for my life, what I chose was to continue with all the fun, and as a self-help measure, I did the self-analysis about all of my accomplishments in all stages of my life irrespective of any size either small or big doesn't matter to assess the amount of efforts and hard work I will have to put in more even if it will take sleepless days and nights to work on something that is going to change the taste of my life forever having beautiful purpose.

KANIKA SINHA

Let's say, if you are a fitness freak and loves doing yoga or any other fitness style than, just the way breathing looks simple and easy but doing any yoga postures in full form can be a bit tricky likewise, for most of us reading may look simple and easy but the hardest part can be to execute what we have read and understood. Right?

I too agree with it.But believe me, once you will start seeing the results by putting efforts into something that you genuinely love and care with great amount of patience and perseverance, every single effort will feel like a piece of cake and you will simply pat your back for doing something really right and great with your life. Guaranteed!

So, just like any other form of yoga and meditation technique -

Reading is what you breathe in, and
Acting is what you breathe out!

And, when you will reach your point of alignment of mind, heart, and soul by doing this form of yoga and meditation technique or applying the knowledge that you will read or learn through this book, that's when the serenity will prevail and you will begin living your beautiful life with an intense amount of happiness and contentment in any stage of your life.

While on my life journey, I came across, some of the more powerful ingredients or words that also contributed well in shaping my thought process –

Start where you are,
Use what you have
Do what you can!
ARTHUR ASHE

It's not the color of our skin,
It's the color of our thoughts that makes us different!
STEVEN AITCHISON

Hard work beats talent
When talent doesn't work hard
TIM NOTKE

Every small or big accomplishment begins with the decision to try!
Unknown

So, I truly believe –

Words does work as one of the strongest sources for guiding and developing our mind if we believe in the power of self-help through self-learning and development process !

© LIFE PHOTOGRAPHY

There were times, when I was also looking for help from successful mentors or life coaches and realized the fact that my tight budget was not allowing me to ask for professional help and was imposing boundaries and limitation to my high aspirations.

If you or any of your known friends or family member is undergoing similar situations, than you should not feel disappointed, as I understand that despite of having money, we sometimes cannot hire them because it can cost us too high and can hit our pockets heavily.

Since, I loved reading and writing as well, so I decided to create my own dictionary of powerful words as shared in earlier sections of this book that can work just like reliable mentors, guide, or teacher or as an accountability partner to push my mental limits at par believing –

One best book is equal to hundred good friends but one good friend is equal to a library !
(APJ Abdul Kalam)

Having the same thought process, I created my own dictionary of powerful words that helped me to stay on my absolute track because even if we are on the right track and are just sitting back and doing nothing, we can drown at some point in our life.

Now, are you wondering how much deep faith I have in powerful words and how they can be one our best mentor, guide, or friend?

Let's try to understand why do I believe so?

I tried almost everything I was passionate about through the series of trials so that, I could educate, enlighten, and empower myself with the right amount of knowledge and can create the right career path with more clarity and a focused mind.

While I tried everything, I still felt that I was lacking a sense of direction as in which direction I should utilize my creative energies in, in the best possible way so that others can also get benefit through my life so as a result another best cooking or life tip that I learned was –

In the series of trials, you can find right direction of trials !

© LIFE PHOTOGRAPHY

Hence, *"TRY"* is one of my favorite word from the world of English language that changed my internal world and gave me meaningful directions and an unlimited amount of opportunities to convert all my wasteland into wonderland by exploring and expanding my universal limits in different areas of life to shape my best *self* so, I honestly and sincerely believe that words do have the power to help us as a mentor, because if I wouldn't have tried anything using all other ingredients, I wouldn't have touched the ground surface of an artistic ocean inside me and would not have created the better **SELF** that I am today.

Let me give you a classic example of Terry Fox, a Canadian athlete, humanitarian, and cancer research activist with one amputated leg due to cancer, is the best inspiring symbol of hope and courage, extraordinary optimistic and never-give-up attitude and whose actions and words inspired millions of minds, hearts, and souls:

> *"I just wish people should realize that anything*
> *is possible because dreams are made if people try"*

So, while exploring my artistic world through just one word called "TRY", another interesting cooking or life tip that I learned was —

If you have a worm called TRY you can achieve anything you put your Mind, Heart and Soul into !

©LIFE PHOTOGRAPHY

Now, it could be possible that while you are executing too many words at the same time you may feel little exhaustive with your energies, so to recharge yourself take a look at more ingredients that worked just like energy boosters for me during all of my accomplishments so far just like the desserts of any scrumptious meal.

CHAPTER – V

Stay motivated to live your soul purpose

Now, once you have met your "self" or have discovered the true purpose of your soul than, while giving your best if at any point of time you feel less energetic you can always recharge your batteries with some powerful energy boosters giving instant positive energies to recharge your undying spirit.

- *Speak five affirmations to yourself every morning:*
    1. *I can do it*
    2. *God is always with me*
    3. *I can be the winner If I continue to persist until that "ONE DAY"*
    4. *Today is my day*

- *A smooth sea never made a skilled sailor.*
- *When nothing is sure, everything is possible (Margaret Drabble)*
- *Never stop learning because life never stops teaching (Unknown)*

- *Until you spread your wings, you will have no idea how far you can fly (Unknown)*
- *The greatest pleasure in life is doing what people say you cannot do (Unknown)*
- *You have to fight through some bad days to earn the best days of your life (Unknown)*
- *The greatest glory in living lies not in never falling, but in rising every time we fall (Nelson Mandela)*
- *Waves are inspiring, not because they rise and fall, but because they never fail to rise again (Unknown)*
- *Great things take time, be kind and patient enough until you sail through successfully (Unknown)*
- *Life is like a camera, Focus on whats important, Capture the good times, Develop from the negatives and if things don't work out take another shot (Unknown)*
- *You are not going to master the rest of your life in one day, just relax, master the day, than just keep doing that every day (Unknown)*
- *You will be victorious in anything or everything if you love doing it. Just keep the passion alive (Kanika Sinha)*

Now, that you have all of the essential ingredients to create the healthiest dreamlife recipe for yourself and your loved ones what are you waiting for?

Let's welcome the new life with an open arm to embrace the new version of yourself to make rest of your life the best of your life with fullest zest.

Remember, life is a journey. No one is ahead of you or behind you. You are not more or less enlightened than others, we are where we exactly need to be. We all are teachers and we all are students, so don't stop doing, trying, learning, fighting, or experimenting until innovation or miracle happens through continuous self-learning and development process thinking universe as your limit.

Fall in love with taking care of yourself. Fall in love with becoming the best version of yourself, but with patience, compassion and with respect of your own journey.

Between yesterday's mistakes and tomorrow's hope, there is a fantastic opportunity called today. Live it! Love it! because life is yours!

I know, one of the question that must be coming to your mind is, how to memorize the entire list of powerful words? Ha – Ha!

Well, the answer is simple, the best way you can do so is, to start trying or doing something that you love in your everyday life because the more you will try or practice what you love doing, the more you will become one of the best example of walking dictionary and you can always feel confident in every stage of your life to create or remain as one of the best versions of all the time to live this single blessed life beautifully.

So, try implementing the knowledge that you have learned through this book in your own life with sincere and optimistic attitude to be your best version and to inspire other people as much as much as you can believing, sharing is caring.

CHAPTER – VI

Spread your optimistic energies at Universe level

Once you have reached your intended destination by pursuing the below equation of life –

Passion => Purpose => Dream => Actions => Create => Achieve => Share => Inspire => X – Ordinary self => MEANINGFUL LIFE

Than,

> *Tell the story of the mountains that you climbed or ocean that you swimmed because your words could become a page in someones else survival guide !*
>
> *- Morgan Harper Nichols*

Share with your friends and family members if you want to see them happy too as a compassionate human being and as a generous step towards joining me on my journey of helping people as much as we can.When you cook any authentic recipe of your life passionately with some purpose to convert any of your dream recipes into reality through your actions; to achieve sense of accomplishment than, we should also try to share the ingredients in some ways with the people at large to inspire them to change the taste of their life too to help them create better or best version of their authentic self and to live a meaningful life ahead compassionately in all other areas of life too.

So, If your actions inspire others to dream more, learn more, do more and become more you are a leader and with that said you should try sharing your successful stories and ingredients with the outside world too because when you share your doings with the outside world than your level of happiness and contentment gets multiplied and goes 10x up from your original level and raises your confidence at much higher level too.

Once you start your adventurous journey through the self- learning and development process, you can simply start by implementing the knowledge acquired from this book at any current stage of your life and if you think this book has helped you in some way to become your better or best version, has helped you to achieve even the smallest dreams of your life, has shaped your life and has brought a big *smile* on your face than, do write and share your experiences with me at my email id **selfprogresslife@gmail.com** to help me fulfill another dream of mine.

If you are looking for more information to overcome any other challenges or obstacles or problems in any areas of your life than, do share and drop me an email describing your concerns to help you with the best creative solutions and to improve the taste, quality and dimensions of your life to my best.

Please feel free to write me, thinking that we are one team that needs love and support from each other to create special bond of relationship lifelong, to enjoy versatile flavors of life, to make our whole existence worthwhile on this earth and to make our victory viable.

Imagine how incredible you would be one day if you start fantasizing about the better life and start building the one.

Life always offers you a second chance, It's called tomorrow so, start sketching your dreams now with something that you love doing the most in your life and which can help you see your new best version beyond imagination.

Hope you like my share of learning curves and experiences as I really hope that they should help you too to create your life story by converting all your dreams into reality to spread universal peace.

And, at last but not the least, would like to thank you for spending your valuable time in reading my book, as I truly believe that your life will never be the same again if you keep doing what you love passionately every single day because it is not the color of your skin, not the texture of your hairs, not the size and shape of your body, not the height or anything else outside, but is inside, that helps you to connect with the universe and that's true *PASSION for your PURPOSE* so,

Find your true passion, define your highest purpose, take actions to innovate or invent your new authentic SELF and to convert all your dreams into reality to live a meaningful life ahead boosting self - growth and development at personal and universe level!

If an Egg is broken by outside force, Life Ends,
If Broken by Inside force, Life Begins,
Great Things Always Begin from Inside

Trust your journey it will be worth it !

Here's wishing you all the success ahead to live the best dream life ever that you think that you deserve at your best, to inspire people as much as you can and to live your life in the most unique way as universe helps to those who takes pride in everything, they love to do so just TRY because,

Get motivated, to discover the true passion of your life,

Get motivated, to discover the true purpose of your life,

Get motivated, to be the artists of your life,

Get motivated, to be the greatest being of your life,

KANIKA SINHA

Get motivated, to be the most authentic self of your life,

Get motivated, to stay motivated all your life,

Get motivated, to create your life your way,

Get motivated, to live your life your way,

Get motivated, to live all your dreams,

Get motivated, to inspire people to live their dreams,

Get motivated, to spread love, joy, peace and

prosperity in your own life and others life,

Get motivated, to live a content and successful

life with fullest enthusiasm all your life!

CHAPTER – VII

Express your strong belief system to work like Logo of your life

Your Smile is a logo

Your personality is your business card

How you leave others feeling after an interaction becomes your trademark!

The symbol or logo of my life that you are seeing right now was created using my two favorite colors Red and Orange wherein,

RED indicates PASSION and ORANGE indicates ENTHUSIASM or UPLIFTMENT!

The two powerful colors or words were blended well to express my belief system.

So, if you too want to live a happy and content life, uplift yourself to uplift others passionately by doing something that you love doing the most every day to live your life with fullest enthusiasm always wherever you travel in this world!

That's the beauty of living an authentic LIFE with your powerful authentic self.

Please find below the given link to access my page easily from anywhere in the world by just using your internet services -

https://www.facebook.com/LIFE-Live-It-with-Fullest-Enthusiasm34-108436616227449/

And, don't forget to like and share my page with others for spreading love, joy and optimism and to connect with me directly through my public account "LIFE – Live it with fullest Enthusiasm34" on Facebook and life_live_it_to_the-fullest34 as Kanika Sinha (Nika) on Instagram if you enjoyed reading my book to receive more information or knowledge as part of my continued growth and development rest of my life.

YOU WILL BE BEGINNING YOUR VOYAGE OF DISCOVERY SHORTLY!

TREAT IT AS AN ADVENTURE AND MAY YOU AND YOUR LIFE NEVER BE THE SAME AGAIN!

Let the Magic Begin!

With Gratitude

Kanika Sinha

Life Coach

NURTURE YOUR MIND...

NURTURE YOUR SELF...

TO

LIVE YOUR LIFE WITH FULLEST ENTHUSIASM ALWAYS!

Love & Light
Kanika ☺